FAT
BOY
SWIM
CATHERINE
FORDE
D0300763

Also by Catherine Forde from Egmont

The Drowning Pond
Fifteen Minute Bob
Skarrs
Sugarcoated
Tug of War
Firestarter

FAT
BOY
SWIM
CATHERINE
FORDE
EGMONT

ur faith.
To Mum for your tablet and more.

EGMONT
We bring stories to life

First published in Great Britain 2003
This edition published 2015
by Egmont UK Limited
The Yellow Building, 1 Nicholas Road, London W11 4AN

ISBN 978 1 4052 7931 4

www.egmont.co.uk
www.cathyforde.co.uk

A CIP catalogue record for this title is available from the British Library

Typeset by Avon DataSet Limited, Bidford on Avon, Warwickshire

Printed and bound in Great Britain by the CPI Group

41218/19

CONTENTS

DESSERTS

BITTER SWEETS

NIBBLES

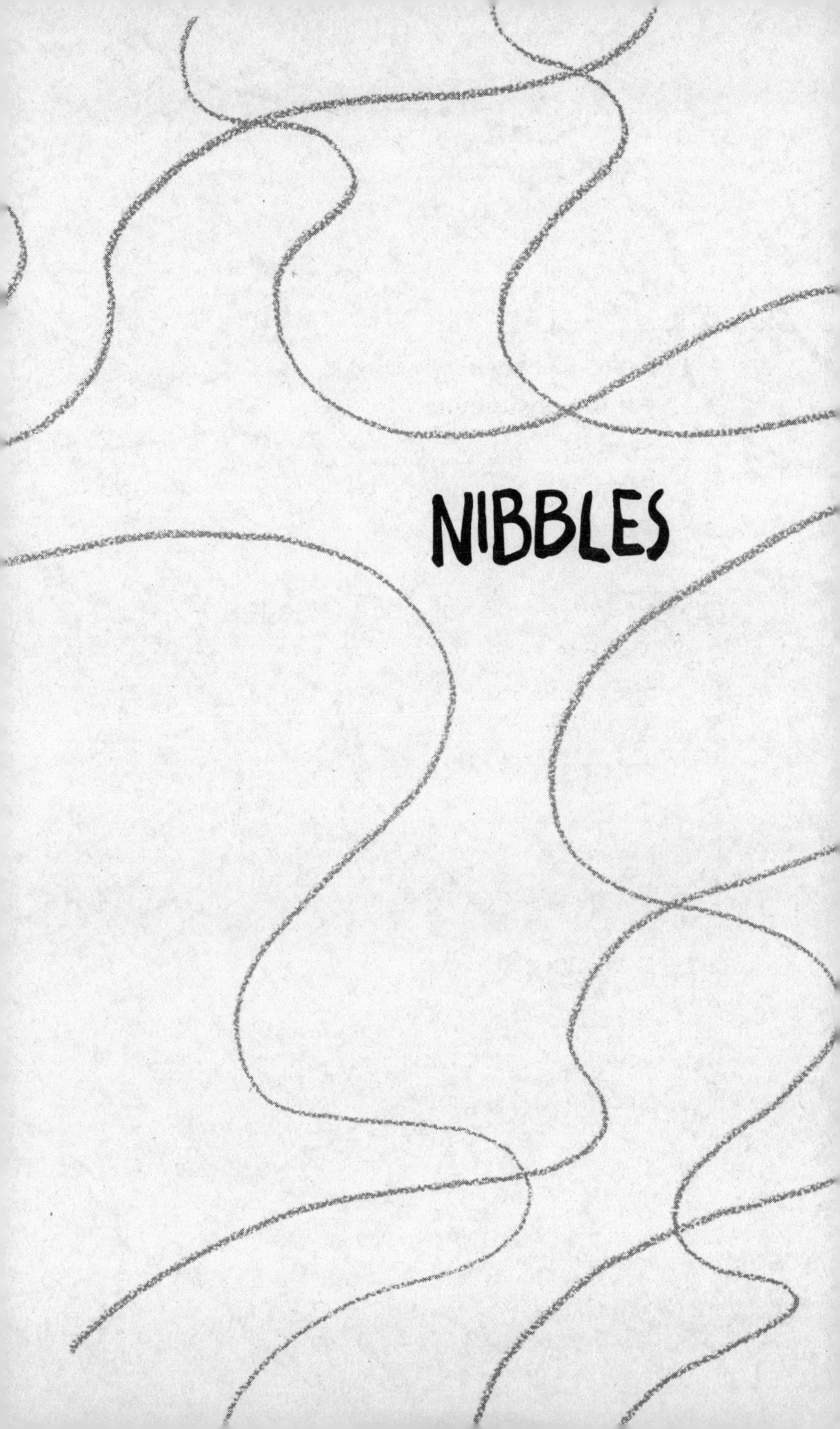

CHAPTER 1
FAT BOY FAT

'Oi, boobsy. Move your fat butt! We're under pressure here.'

One rasp from Maddo McCormack in goals was enough to set Jimmy stumbling up the pitch, as though someone had given him a wedgie up the backside.

He only shuffled half a dozen steps, each one making his thick flesh judder. The impact of his foot hitting the ground had him wheezing like an old accordion.

It was hopeless. Pointless. Jimmy halted. Leaned forward, hands on knees.

Gasping.

Knackered.

Somewhere to his left he could hear the flat clack of hockey sticks as the girls played their interschool final. Voices rose through the heat and drifted across to the field where Jimmy panted.

Summer sounds.

He hated them.

This summer was off to a bad start. For Jimmy anyway.

Unlike most years it hadn't crept in: one wee glimpse of sun in April, followed by three weeks of rain and back on with the winter clothes, bit of snow in May, then a disappointing June.

First of May this year, a furnace-blast of sunshine had scorched the west of Scotland. Day after day after day of stifling heat. Night after sleepless stuffy night. Even the ice-cream vans struggled to chime through the thick air.

After two months of weather like this, Jimmy felt he was suffocating under his own sticky weight. Made worse because it was serious school sports season. No getting out of it.

At least today's match was the pay-off for eight weeks of peace.

Blow the whistle, Jimmy willed Hamblin, the ref. It had to be full-time, otherwise he'd never have been forced from the sanctuary of the subs' bench. Although

St Jude's insisted that every pupil had a stint on the field, it was unspoken policy that Jimmy Kelly was only played in the dying moments of a game, and only then if St Jude's were winning.

They'd been 2-1 up when Jimmy went on.

Blow the whistle. Jimmy panted, lungs struggling to inhale enough air to let him straighten up, let alone move.

'Jimmy!'

'Jimmy!! **J-i-i-i-m-m-y!!!**'

His name came hurtling towards him, screeched at maximum volume. A primitive chant. Carrying the threat – no, the *promise* – that he'd be ripped apart if he didn't snap to it.

He had to look up. Wasn't going to get away with playing the invisible hulk.

'Never mind them, moron. Get your eye on that ball! Kick it back up the pitch, Kelly. It's at your feet, man!'

GI Joe was level with Jimmy on the sideline, eyeballing him. His proximity didn't make him lower his voice any. He bawled as though his lungs would burst.

'Come on, big man. Chase that ball. Boot it up the

field. He's on your back. Aaach!!! What you playing at?'

Jimmy's head went down. But that didn't matter. He could see what GI Joe was doing without looking. Swinging his whole body round from left to right in utter despair. Like he always did when he tried to get Jimmy to shift. Shaking his head in dismay was never enough. Every bit of him had to join in.

Jimmy knew GI Joe's face would be beetroot, wriggly veins bulging from his temples under the line where his bristly crewcut began. His forehead would throb visibly from the effort of screeching down the field at Jimmy.

Later, when GI Joe tried to speak at normal pitch, his voice would crack. If you didn't know what kind of bloke Coach was you might think he'd been bubbling.

Jimmy knew – again without having to look up – that even the charitable guys in defence were throwing him daggers over their shoulders as the play moved off up the field. Muttering curses under their breath. Wanting Jimmy taken off once and for all.

Others were more straightforward with their objections.

'What's the balloon up to? Ball right at him and he lets it past.'

'Blinkin' liability. Shouldnae let him on full stop.'

'Whales canny play fitba'.'

Jimmy stopped moving.

Might as well have been a universe away, the lot of them. He'd never catch up.

'Kick it back up. **NAW.** Up the way! **UP** the way!'

They were all at it now.

A dozen voices. Subs on the bench leaping up and down behind GI Joe. The rest of his side charging towards him. Circling like vultures.

'Here, Kelly.'

'Here, big man.'

'Straight back up to me. **Hurry.**'

Flustered, Jimmy could barely tell one team from the other, the oppo just clones of his own side clad in different jerseys. All he knew was sweat on hungry faces, saliva stringing from open mouths as two thundering teams descended on him.

Nightmare.

'KICK IT NOW KELLY!'

Even Jimmy couldn't ignore that voice scaling two octaves in his ear, or the clasped entreaty of GI Joe's Cumberland sausage fingers under his nostrils. He'd have to make contact with that football. After all, it was sauntering almost casually in his direction as though it was out for a wee stroll on the pitch.

All Jimmy had to do was . . .

He gulped. Straightened up, searching the panting faces in the closing semicircle before him.

There was Victor.

Star player.

Captain.

He'd aim for Victor.

Jimmy drew back his left foot, approximated a kick and – *oof* – was felled like an oak. His own defence had surged as one to tackle the nifty mover from the opposition who had sussed it would be tomorrow before Jimmy's boot touched that football. But it was too late. A superb slide kick shunted the ball just enough towards Maddo's goal mouth where the opposition striker was poised.

BAM.

On side.

'Game over. Good effort lads. 'Way and congratulate the oppo now.'

Hamblin, ref duties over, spat his whistle at Jimmy. Almost reluctantly, he peeled back the scrum champing menacingly over the clammy flesh-mound lying winded on the grass.

Extending his long arms, Hamblin corralled the mob away, steering it towards the middle of the pitch. Beyond lynching distance of Jimmy.

Not once, however, did Hamblin check any of the insults his pupils hurled like clods over his shoulders in Jimmy's direction. Not even when Victor jooked round him and crowed, ***'Fat Boy Fat'***, to an accompanying volley of gobs and laughter.

Hamblin was too busy scowling at Jimmy himself.

'Bloody cup lost on aggregate. Useless butterball shouldnae be allowed anywhere near a pitch.'

CHAPTER 2

CHANGING ROOM

Jimmy waited behind on the pitch, wishing the grass could swallow him up, even for a while. Flat on his back, he stared at the blue, blue sky until he felt recovered enough to examine the mucky trench Victor Swift's stud had gouged in his shin after the final tackle.

That's for starters, fatso.

Best wait a bit.

Let the others get changed.

After all, he wouldn't be missed.

The PE block felt deserted as Jimmy entered. He allowed himself to relax a little.

Could have been worse, thought Jimmy. If it hadn't

been a Friday afternoon, Hamblin might have been tempted to repeat last year's humiliation. Forcing Jimmy into the showers. Trying to compensate the rest of the team after Jimmy's crucial own goal.

'Everyone will sit quietly on the benches – *quietly,* I said, McCormack – until Kelly has showered and dressed. You'll all be dismissed when he's nice and clean for his mammy.'

A year on Jimmy still squirmed at the recollection. Having to shower naked. Whole team watching. Hearing their snorts and laughter over the running water. Maddo blowing up his cheeks. Victor slapping them flat with great farting noises that sent the other lads into hysterics.

'Sir, Kelly needs all they showers on. He's only wettin' one of his bum cheeks.'

'You missed a bit you canny see, fatso . . .'

'I didnae know you got red-haired whales . . .'

'Ah can see Kelly's tinky-winky . . .'

'Sir, this is putting me aff ma dinner . . .'

After the shower, the further indignity of having to towel off and dress. Then clamber into giant underpants, sweaty fingers fumbling to button the trousers and failing to so. Jimmy feeling the mass of his belly mash against the material.

Sticky.

Clumsy.

Hopeless.

Hamblin had leaned against the door of the changing room, tapping his whistle against his teeth in that annoying way of his. Whenever Jimmy glanced up he was trawling the reactions of the team with his hard blue eyes. Thin smile on his face.

Sorry about today, lads, but this'll cheer you up.

Only when Jimmy was struggling with his shoelaces, all the blood rushing up to his head as he bent over, Maddo poking him in the backside and going *boingggg,* had Hamblin let the others go.

'Show's over lads.'

Anything but that today, decided Jimmy.

And he had timed it well. All that was left of the team was the muck they'd trailed in from the pitch for the cleaners. Clumps of slimy mud with bits of grass sticking out like sparse hair pockmarked the floor. Empty cans and plastic bottles, none of them upright, littered the benches. Dods of chewing gum stuck to the walls. And then there was the smell. The fug of deodorant catching Jimmy's throat and irritating his chest couldn't mask it. Nor could the tang of the putrid pink carbolic Hamblin insisted the boys lather up with in the showers. Even the sweet echoes of the hair gel the lads used to get their fringes spiked up like the singer from the well-cool band they all liked wasn't camouflage enough.

What was the smell exactly? Earth, and sweat and dirt. A boy smell. A team smell. Shared activity. Belonging.

It was a smell that made Jimmy hungry.

Jimmy heard water running. He picked his way across the muddy floor to the showers. Sighed. One shower had been left on full, its jet angled just so to soak the clothes bundled underneath it. Jimmy's school socks were wedged into the shower drain, blocking it so that several inches of scummy water swirled between Jimmy and the shower tap. In that water, among floating islands of hair-balls and discarded sticking plasters, sailed the contents of Jimmy's schoolbag: textbooks, jotters, diary. And his shoes. The schoolbag itself dangled upside down from a high window ledge.

He was an expert by now, was Jimmy, at concentrating on the task in hand. That way he didn't allow himself to dwell on reasons *why* things happened. You focused on the moment and when it had passed, you forgot about it. Moved on. Aunt Pol taught him that. Said it worked for her.

Jimmy used this technique today, stepping into the blocked shower still wearing his football boots, and trying – at least – to save the textbooks from more damage. The jotters had already begun to shred in his hands, but luckily they were the ones he'd finished with this year. Mum liked to keep them.

But the books . . .

Jimmy laid them on the benches, wondering if they would dry out. They were for fourth year English. Mrs Hughes had handed them out today for holiday reading: *Look after them, now.*

His blazer was also for fourth year. And fifth. And sixth, gulped Jimmy, holding the dripping garment at arm's length and turning off the shower. Less than a month old, specially made because of the size. No way would Mum be able to fork out for another.

Jimmy forced himself not to think about these problems. They belonged to the future. For now he had to deal with getting himself and his drenched belongings home. His travel pass, somewhere in his blazer pocket, was pulped beyond recognition.

Awkward in studs, wet bundle leaving a trail behind him, Jimmy began the long walk home. He kept his head down when he passed the staffroom, praying he was invisible.

But he didn't slip past the staffroom unnoticed, although there was only one person left on such a fine Friday afternoon in June.

And GI Joe wasn't a proper teacher anyway.

STARTERS

CHAPTER 3
TABLET

Fired up for bingo, Mum didn't look twice at the sopping wet bundle that Jimmy dumped in the bath. However, she wasn't so keen to get out that she failed to clock Jimmy wearing his football gear. She tailed him from drawer to cupboard to bedside cabinet as he rummaged for the inhaler he needed when his chest felt extra tight.

'What you doing playing football in a heat wave, son? Look at the colour of your face. What d'you think that doctor's letter's for? And what're you looking for? Those? That?'

'This,' gasped Jimmy, sucking gratefully on the inhaler.

Just leave me, Mum, he wanted to blurt in her face. *Let me get sorted. Empty my bag. Football's over till fourth year. No point thinking about it till then.*

'Going out?' he asked her, as if he was daft. She went out every Friday. 'Look at you all dressed up.'

She wasn't, of course. All she'd done was remove her housecoat and run a comb through her hair.

'Och, away,' Mum smiled, primping at the attention. 'Bingo down St Jude's. Murder in this heat. Pol'll be here straight from work. You'll get something to eat?'

Halfway out of the front door, Mum hesitated.

'You take it easy, son. You can't overdo things like other folk.'

Bliss. Peace. Place to myself. Jimmy sighed, relaxing at last.

She meant well, Mum, but she was always fussing. Flapping around him like a nervous crow on amphetamines: *Don't do this. Don't do that.* You'd think he was a blinking invalid. Didn't she get it by now?

He was just fat.

Lardy.

Ginormous.

Clinically obese . . .

'Don't start that again,' Jimmy warned himself

aloud, but it was tough. Soon as he got thinking about it, he had a fight on his hands to stop his mind from scrolling down the litany of names for fat that he'd been called over the years. Must be hundreds of them, maybe even thousands.

'Just words. Ignore them. Switch off. Walk away,' Aunt Pol had taught Jimmy many years ago, and to a certain extent, he had learned to follow her advice. He shrugged off insults. *Sticks and stones* and all that.

But inside, deep inside, it blooming hurt. Every time.

Inside, Jimmy didn't feel like Smelly Kelly, Fat Boy Fat. Of course not. He was just – a teenager. Normal in every way. Apart from his size. His bedroom was a pit. His feet stank. He hated getting up on school mornings. If any of his classmates scratched away a layer or two of fat they'd find a teenage heart like theirs beating for Britney or Kylie or Pink or Shakira. If any of his classmates ever bothered to *talk* to him, instead of slagging him off, they'd find he was just as clued up as they were on films, on books, on telly, even on sport. And as for music . . .

Jimmy sighed. It was Friday night after all. Why

dwell on things he couldn't change?

He flicked through the growing tower of CDs he was constructing under Aunt Pol's guidance. An edifice, she called it, combining the best of the old and new millennium.

'Try this. Try that,' she'd say.

Beatles at the foundation, naturally. Then Motown, soul, and glam, and blues, and ska, and punk, even country. A bit of everything, in fact. Not forgetting her Friday favourite: Abba.

How could Jimmy possibly dwell on the football fiasco or zero friend count when 'Dancing Queen' filled the flat? Aunt Pol's tune. He could see her already, catching the song's first jangling arpeggio from the bottom of the close, and dancing her way up three flights of stairs, arms waving above her head, lyrics tumbling from her big red mouth.

Just the thought of her, way over the top, grabbing Jimmy's hands and birling him into the middle of the hall, was enough to delete all the misery of the afternoon. Aunt Pol always made Jimmy feel good. For a while at least.

*

Everything was under control in the kitchen. Jimmy had crushed garlic, zested a lime, added some of his basil-infused olive oil and roasted the past-it peppers lying in the fridge.

He was just rolling out the pasta for his home-made feta ravioli, singing, in a painful falsetto, a descant to the descending chorus of 'The Winner Takes it All' (his favourite Abba track, although he kept quiet about that), when he heard Aunt Pol's familiar cry:

'What *is* that smell?'

The ritual never changed. Jimmy knew, without turning to look, that Aunt Pol was in the flat. A flurry of her scent flowered the kitchen before she reached it herself. Joy. Mum treated her to a new spray every Christmas. Jimmy loved it. Loved it so much that he'd slip out into the hall while Aunt Pol was busy poking and tasting the contents of every pot and pan on the cooker to fill his lungs from her sweet slipstream. He'd take his time, moving Aunt Pol's high heels from the front door where she always kicked them off, picking up her bag from where she always dropped it in her haste to see him. Then he'd serve up dinner.

Aunt Pol's reaction was part of the ritual, too.

'This food is just . . . I mean it's so . . .'

There was no need for Aunt Pol to struggle for an adjective to describe Jimmy's efforts.

Divine would do.

He knew, as sure as he was a plab on the pitch and a joke in the gym, that he was a star in the firmament of the kitchen. Jimmy just knew. Always had. How to cook. Brilliantly. When to go easy on the butter. When to add an extra egg white. When to stop stirring a sauce. How long to beat a batter.

Tablet – which Jimmy made every Friday night – was his *pièce de résistance,* but **everything** he made tasted like ambrosia. Not Ambrosia Creamed Rice, but ambrosia: food of the gods.

Aunt Pol mopped her plate with a slice of Jimmy's fennel bread. 'Betcha,' she said, 'folk are sitting in poncy restaurants right now paying through the nose for grub that doesn't come near what you make, Jim.'

She was the only person who ever called him that. Never Jimmy.

'I'm not too full. I'm not bloated. Flavours were magic and here, you just *chucked* this together from stuff lying around.'

Aunt Pol always analysed Jimmy's cooking. Only time she grew serious. Unless Jimmy was getting grief somewhere. Then she grew seriously serious.

When she discussed cooking with Jimmy, she did so with a mixture of admiration and incomprehension. Sometimes, Jimmy even thought she looked upset. As if she had something difficult to say, but choked her words back down.

'Can't believe you've been born with this talent,' she'd say. 'Certainly don't get it from me.'

'I'm good, amn't I?' Jimmy would reply, knowing that nothing gave him more pleasure than the sight of someone reduced to an inarticulate sigh because of his genius. Filled him better than any meal.

Made him feel right.

Made him feel happy.

Pity Jimmy's gift had to be kept top secret by Mum and Aunt Pol. Well. He could understand, especially now he was older, why it was best that his genius remained undiscovered. What would folks say, after all, if they discovered that:

Big blob Kelly

Had one special talent.

And it involved food?

God's sick joke that, sighed Jimmy, not for the first time.

Later, in the kitchen, pouring sugar into a pot to melt, Jimmy accepted it was probably best that people didn't know what he could do with food. He'd hate anything to put him off the skill he loved.

Not that he was a flipping martyr either. He was sick of the tablet fiends crowding him at every school fundraiser, never thinking for a minute that he was responsible for the biggest money-spinner on the cake and candy stall.

The urge to blurt out his secret could be overwhelming, especially when he had to watch the very people who accused him of being a lardy guzzler, scoffing several bars of *his* tablet at once. Ripping off the cling-film with greedy hands. Drooling their compliments: 'This stuff's the work of a genius.'

But Jimmy had to bite his tongue and watch the faces of all those who loved to make his life a misery twinkle with delight as he

p – e – e – l – e – d

back – he always did it

r – e – a – l – l – y

slowly for maximum effect – the lid of each plastic tablet-crammed tub.

No wonder he was tempted, when mouths usually twisted into sour jeers were drooling in anticipation for one draught of the sugary buttery magic that he had concocted and cut into neat, more-ish squares, to shout:

'*Oi*! *I made all this. I'm not totally useless, am I*?'

'Not totally useless,' Jimmy rasped aloud, the bitterness in his voice taking him by surprise. He shook his head clear of dark thoughts. Friday night, remember. He'd Aunt Pol to himself, Bowie on the CD, while his huge pot of tablet bubbled on the hob. He'd even sorted the soggy textbooks, having the brainwave of laying them out on the cooker using the dying heat from the oven and the low warmth radiating from the ring where his sugar was melting to dry them out. They'd be fine.

His blazer was another matter, decidedly drookit as it swung above him on the pulley like a giant shapeless bird.

But – ach – he'd the rest of the weekend to worry about it, Jimmy decided, adding condensed milk to his melted sugar and beating the mixture. His tablet would be just the way Father Patrick, the only other person in the world who knew Jimmy's secret, liked it. Still warm, with a soft bite. The old priest's pay-off for walking Mum home from bingo every Friday.

'Cooee!'

Mum was back early, which was strange in itself. Normally she never returned from bingo until Aunt Pol – who thought the sound, let alone the sight of Father Patrick gorging himself on the scrapings of Jimmy's tablet pot, revolting – had woken herself up during the credits of *Frasier*, and gone home.

Not tonight.

Stranger, thought Jimmy from the kitchen, was

the phoney *Are you decent? We've got a visitor* chime in Mum's voice. There was none of that kidmaleery with Father Patrick.

So Jimmy was caught way off-guard when he wandered into the hall, drying his hands on his t-shirt as if everything was normal.

'Heya, Mamma. You'va gotta to trya mya feta ravioli! Ita wasa *magnifico* . . .'

Jimmy's booming Italian greeting dwindled to a squeak. Father Patrick hadn't walked Mum home from the bingo tonight.

''Lo there,' said GI Joe. His voice sounding cracked and hoarse. As though he'd been yelling recently. Jimmy winced at the memory of the afternoon.

'Why would I want to see you?'

To torture me, thought Jimmy, his heart beating unhealthily fast at the mere sight of GI Joe.

He shrugged. Voice glum.

'Dunno . . .'

Extra training, he was thinking. Coach is gonna give me extra training.

'Well, I've been hearing all about you.' GI Joe

jabbed at Jimmy with a squat index finger.

Hamblin, thought Jimmy. He's figured out some keep-fit punishment for me.

Behind GI Joe, Jimmy noticed Mum's eyes widen to a glare, her mouth ruching into a tight purse of disapproval. She was trying to tell him something.

He *had* answered, hadn't he?

'So what have I been hearing about you?'

'Dunno,' Jimmy repeated even more glumly. Looking at Mum's deepening frown he added:

'Sir?'

CHAPTER 4

SPACE INVASION

How the heck was Jimmy supposed to know GI Joe was a priest?

Divine telepathy?

He'd appeared from nowhere in the PE department one day after Easter. Call me Coach, he'd said. Added: 'I'm gonna kick ass.' Hardly an ecclesiastical starter for ten.

'Been watching you jokers.' He'd paced the gym like a hungry rotweiller, eyeballing the team one by one. When he came to Maddo McCormack, he lingered. Stared him out until Maddo – *Maddo*! – looked down. No one did that. Especially not a member of staff.

And here was a *priest* . . .

I mean, thought Jimmy. He's a right hard man.

That's what all the lads said, licking their wounds after GI's first coaching session.

'You're the most diabolical shower I've ever seen,' he'd growled as they scuttled off the pitch with their collective tail between their legs.

No one had escaped punishment that day. Even the guys who played their socks off. Even Victor, the Ronaldo of St Jude's who, since Coach's arrival, was having private after-school training because several premier league teams were angling to give him trials. Ronaldo or not, you got fifty squat jumps for swearing, a hundred press-ups for dirty play, high knee running on the spot for dawdling, two hundred star jumps for standing still . . .

Jimmy, whose gameplan had been to retire early with a quick flash of his inhaler (usually all he had to do was start taking it out of his pocket and Hamblin bawled him to the benches glad to see the back of him), needed three days off attached to his nebuliser after the first training session.

None of them would ever have guessed GI Joe was a priest. Jimmy didn't believe it himself, yet there he was – '*Father* Joseph!' as Mum snapped – holding out his hand for Jimmy to shake. Even dressed as a priest. Jimmy had been in too much shock at the sight of the crewcut at first to notice the dusty black suit you only ever see priests wearing. GI's neck bulged from the stranglehold of a dog-collar.

At least in his holy gear, Coach seemed smaller, less menacingly musclebound. When Jimmy shook GI's hand, he was surprised: the grip, though firm, wasn't the bonecrushing testicle-shrinker that he would have expected.

'Call me Joe.' Coach pumped Jimmy's arm. 'And I know you're Jimmy – or maybe you prefer Jim.'

It didn't matter, Jimmy mumbled, keen to free his hand. He'd a vision of GI Joe flipping him to the ground and standing on his shins until he did fifty sit-ups.

What was GI Joe doing here anyway? Grinning at him like they were suddenly chinas. What was he after?

Before he was any the wiser, Aunt Pol staggered between them mumbling something about the time. Jimmy had forgotten all about her in the shock of finding the coach from hell in his hall.

He knew by the way she was keeping her head

down, bashing past Jimmy as if she was scoring a try, that she was keen to escape.

'Careful, there,' said GI Joe, steadying Aunt Pol's elbow as she bent to pull her sling-back over her heel.

At the sound of GI Joe's voice, Aunt Pol jerked up as if she'd touched an electric fence. Jimmy thought he heard her squeal although it could well have been his own falsetto. Her stiletto had stabbed the fleshiest part of his big toe.

She didn't hang around to apologise, either. Off she shot, tripping downstairs faster than it was safe in peerie heels.

'*That's* the Pauline you were talking about, Maeve?' GI Joe asked Mum, although he wasn't looking at her, Jimmy noticed. His head was cocked towards the open front door, listening to the tap of fading footsteps.

'That's Pauline,' Mum sang, casting her eyes heavenwards. A gesture, thought Jimmy, loaded with what: disapproval? Exasperation?

'Aunt Pol.' Jimmy frowned slightly at Mum. She could be funny about her sister sometimes. Jealous, maybe? Who knows.

'She one of the good guys, Jim?' asked GI Joe. He was studying Jimmy's face as he spoke. Curiously. As if he was seeing him for the first time. Jimmy blushed.

'She's brilliant.'

His reply was fierce; a reflex.

'You take after her, then.'

If Jimmy's ears could have blinked in disbelief they would have done.

Him? Brilliant?

A compliment from the same man who this very day was on his knees, beating the pitch with his fists, screaming: 'Jesus Christ Almighty! An amoeba's got more ball sense, Kelly!' Now the same man was saying, 'Father Patrick said I should talk to you about helping me out with some baking and cooking. Told me to try your tablet.'

Unbelievable, thought Jimmy, staring, gape-mouthed at Mum, who if he wasn't mistaken, was hiding behind GI Joe's broad shoulders. No wonder. She'd betrayed him. To Coach of all people! Didn't she *realise* what he could do with the knowledge that Fat Boy Kelly baked and cooked? This was serving him up a gourmet feast of ammunition to detonate next time Jimmy waddled out the changing room in his PE kit: *Move it, Kelly. You're not icing fairy cakes.*

Moments ticked away. Jimmy's mind too distracted by the prospective torments Mum's disloyalty could wreak on his life, to answer GI Joe.

'Of course Jimmy won't mind helping you, Father,' Mum's voice chimed, small behind the bulk of GI's back. Sacrificing Jimmy now as well as betraying him. Judas!

'Let Father try your tablet.'

'Who's the dark horse, then Jim?' said GI Joe, clamping his hand to Jimmy's shoulder. Out of Mum's earshot, in the tiny kitchen, Jimmy thought he sounded fierce. Jimmy balked. Hated anyone so near him, touching him. He wished GI Joe had stayed in the hall with Mum. He was a space invader in the one place where Jimmy felt happy and safe.

Bitterly, Jimmy cut a sweet square from his newly set batch of tablet and held it out to GI Joe on a knife.

With little interest, GI Joe gulped the offering down in a mouthful.

Wouldn't even have tasted it, thought Jimmy. If Father Patrick had seen him gobble like that he'd have accused GI Joe of sacrilege. You nibbled and sooked each square to make it last.

'I don't have a sweet tooth, Jim, to be honest. But I'm sure this is good stuff,' said GI Joe. Grim, he flicked tablet crumbs into the sink. Father Patrick would have licked every fingertip clean, but Coach seemed more interested in Jimmy's textbooks drying on the cooker. 'You'll be wondering why I'm here,' he said, closing the kitchen door.

His fist lay on the pile of books, clenching and unclenching. 'Gave you a wee fright, eh?'

GI Joe was trying to make Jimmy look at him, crooking his knees slightly to get a better view of Jimmy's downturned face.

No chance. Jimmy buried his jaw against his chins. Say your piece and go. Scrub the palsy-walsy routine.

'I was telling Father Patrick about how the match went today. How there was this big lad in the team. How everyone, including myself, gave him dog's abuse. How he struggled out the changing rooms after everyone had gone home, all his gear soaking. Couldn't get him out of my head, I told Patrick. Great big guy, too, I said. Red hair. You couldn't miss him. Over six feet. Shoulders on him like a swimmer under all that bulk he was carrying. Not to mention, I says, the burden of bullying I saw him take from the team captain downwards. Sight of him shocked me.

'"Och," says Patrick, "That'll be Jimmy. Maeve Kelly's lad. Takes a mighty ribbing, right enough, poor soul. And you can see why, God help him. But here, I'll tell you a wee secret about him: he's worth knowing –" Next thing, Patrick's telling me you've raised a small fortune for St Jude's over the years. Anonymously. That you're a phenomenal cook. And if I'm wanting to run a fundraiser, you're the man.'

Jimmy sank his belly into the kitchen worktop in relief. He almost looked up at GI Joe and smiled. Coach wasn't here to bawl him out or make him do star jumps. He wanted macaroons and meringues. No burpees. No problem. Everything was fine. His secret was safe. All Jimmy had to do was get Mum to make GI Joe promise to keep shtoom.

Jimmy shrugged. 'Write me a list of what you want. How much you need. I'll bake no bother . . .'

THUMP!

SPLOOSH.

GI Joe's fist crashed down on the pile of dried-out textbooks at the same moment a great splat of water landed in Jimmy's hair. And another:

SPLOOSH!

As GI Joe and Jimmy tipped their heads upwards two pendant tears trickled from Jimmy's blazer sleeves on to their faces.

'Get that down from there,' growled GI Joe, snapping his fingers at the pulley. 'You should have reported this, Jim. I'm not just here about your bloody baking.'

GI Joe's voice had risen to its angry football pitch pitch. Instinctively Jimmy glanced towards the kitchen door. Was Mum listening?

'If you're gonna help me, then I'm gonna help you, Jim, else there's no deal,' he said, several decibels more quietly. 'Give us a plastic bag for starters and I'll sort this.'

GI Joe dropped his hand on Jimmy's shoulder. Paw-like, his grip tightening on the flesh until Jimmy was forced to look. He met Coach's gaze.

'Gotta sort yourself, big man. Bloke with swimmer's shoulders like yours.'

GI Joe shook the plastic bag, straining with the wet weight of the blazer, in Jimmy's face.

Jimmy winced at the gesture. How much had GI Joe seen earlier?

'Awright?'

GI dunted Jimmy in the stomach.

'Yes, Father,' said Jimmy feebly.

'Coach,' GI corrected him. 'Two o'clock tomorrow. St Jude's.'

CHAPTER 5

THE SHADOW SHAPE AND THE DREAM

4 a.m.

Light outside.

Jimmy had been awake for hours, watching dawn break through his open window.

He sneezed. A huge hay fever sneeze. Sneezed again. He kicked away the sheet entangling him and let one leg flop over the side of his bed. Its weight dragged uncomfortably on his spine and he heaved it back on to the mattress again with a sigh. His body was slick with sweat. It prickled his scalp, darkening the hair around his ears and temples.

If it hadn't been for the dream he'd have gone back to sleep by now.

It was a crazy dream – always worse after a bad day.

His recurring swimming pool dream.

And that was crazy for starters.

Jimmy couldn't swim . . .

Not that he hadn't given it a shot. Mum had enrolled him in Little Minnows at four. Kitted him out in age ten trunks and a set of adult armbands. She wasn't happy about it either. Jimmy – a hefty six stone in those days – was delicate, she said. It was Aunt Pol who persuaded her otherwise.

What harm can it do him? I know heavy people who make great swimmers.

Mum had insisted on taking Jimmy poolside, the only parent. Ridiculous in her blue showercap shoe-covers, she asked the nearest boy if Jimmy could squeeze in.

'Nuh. He's a fatty,' four-year-old Victor Swift had said, blowing a wet raspberry and sidling as far away from Jimmy as he could get. As though fatness was catching.

Soon as the teacher's back was turned, Victor pitched Jimmy into the pool.

Later, Jimmy was asked to leave Little Minnows. There were complaints from parents because Jimmy kept swallowing too much water and throwing up on the floats. Still, Aunt Pol kept the pressure on Mum to find a class which would suit.

None of them did. Jimmy was uncoordinated. He couldn't bear to put his face under the water. Whenever he was forced to let go of the side he hyperventilated, thrashing in terror until he sank.

'That's it,' Mum decided after Jimmy was finally stretchered to an ambulance. 'What are we doing? Jimmy's never going to be a swimmer. *You* don't swim. *I* don't swim. *Dad* didn't swim.'

Yet Dad was always in Jimmy's swimming dream. A quarter of the way up the pool. Fully dressed, in his old cardi and slippers. Sitting in his big winged chair. Newspaper up to his nose the way Jimmy remembered him: *Do Not Disturb*. There was even a cloud of cigarette smoke above his head, and in some dreams Jimmy could smell the tobacco. Made him cough in his sleep.

The pool in Jimmy's dream was very, very long. It was brightly lit, full of noise. Not sharp, up-close noise, but distant echoey sound. Jumbled words and phrases drifted towards Jimmy from the deep end. Spoken by people too far away to see clearly. Jimmy wished he could reach these shadowy people. There was somebody important up there he had to meet. Someone he didn't know. A Shadow Shape.

Jimmy had never reached the deep end in his dream. And every time he failed, he grew more convinced that when he *did* get there, his life would click into place.

That was why this was such an anxious dream. Why, when it recurred it left him so exhausted, so disappointed.

In the dream tonight, GI Joe clutched Jimmy by the shoulder, blowing a whistle in his ear to start him swimming. Father Patrick was there too, like a great black crow, guzzling a plate of tablet secreted under his cassock.

'Go! Go!' GI Joe shrieked as Jimmy plunged his head under the water. 'You've got swimmer's shoulders, Jim.'

Jimmy lunged forward, passing Aunt Pol in the spectator's gallery. She always watched his dream swims, chewing worriedly on her red nails. Even underwater, he could sense her willing him on:

You'll get there, Jim. Keep going.

And he tried. Ploughing forward with every ounce of strength in his shoulders. Even in sleep he could feel the sinews in his neck strain with the effort. Hear himself grunt. Kick to gain enough momentum to propel himself towards his goal.

One stroke. That was all he managed, all he ever managed. Out as far as Dad in his armchair, never beyond.

Jimmy, floundering like a toad in a muddy puddle, was going nowhere. Arms circled, legs jerked, chin strained forward, but it was hopeless. Always hopeless. He wallowed in the treacle of his dream and the people in the distance receded beyond his view. Their voices evaporated, words becoming whispers he couldn't catch.

The spectator's gallery emptied; everyone gone home.

'Wait!'

Jimmy tried to call out, aware of his mouth opening and shutting in his sleep, but he might as well have been a Little Minnow for all the sound he produced. In the dark of his bedroom, he stretched his hand out in front of him to snatch the dream. Make it stay. But it was fading.

Far away, in the horizon of the dream, there was a stir of movement. The scantest shift that senses could detect.

'Wait.'

The whisper of a shape rose. Big, wide, tall. The Shadow Shape. It was there. But it was leaving.

'Wait!'

Turning. The transparency was turning. It had heard.

But, as usual, Jimmy's own feeble croak had roused him from sleep. And chased the dream away.

CHAPTER 6

THE HUNGRY HOLE

The failure of Jimmy's dream lay on him like something rotten he had eaten. He felt wretched, a washed-out rag. The dream always left him like this. Miserable. Even more fit for nothing than usual. And starving.

Normally, Saturdays were magic. The day was an official diet-free zone as far as Aunt Pol was concerned, no matter how strictly she had been keeping tabs on what Mum let Jimmy eat all week. Jimmy usually went round to Aunt Pol's for a second breakfast. He'd make pancakes on her tiny cooker and they'd drink frothed-up hot chocolates covered in marshmallows until it was time to go out for lunch.

Not today.

Jimmy left a lie on Aunt Pol's machine. Said his hay

fever was bad. She'd hear his voice from her bed. She'd know exactly what he was doing. He'd have to face her later. But, for now, he couldn't help himself.

Armed with a six-pack of crisps, a giant Yorkie and a packet of chocolate digestives, Jimmy thudded down on the settee in front of the telly. He made sure his three cans of Irn Bru were lined up within hand's reach.

How else was he expected to plug the Hungry Hole that the dream had excavated?

When he answered the door several hours later, the dry cleaning fumes from the blazer swinging on GI Joe's finger made his head reel.

'Good as new,' said GI Joe. 'Got it steamed at my auntie's laundry.'

'Thanks,' murmured Jimmy, woozy, his mouth viscid with chocolate. He had completely forgotten his appointment with Coach.

'You should've said if you'd something better on.' GI Joe stepped into the flat. Flummoxed, Jimmy did what Mum said he should always do when a visitor came. He showed GI Joe into the front room.

A witness to Jimmy's shame, even GI Joe didn't seem to know where to look at first, his eyes swivelling in disbelief from Jimmy himself – who had Sugar Puffs velcroed to his t-shirt, warting his face – to the debris-strewn site of Jimmy's latest pig-out.

There were Pringles cartons crushed on the floor, crisp crumbs on the cushions. A carpet of sweetie papers radiating outwards from flicking distance of the spot where Jimmy had sprawled for the last four hours. Propped against the remote was a giant Cadbury's Dairy Milk with the wrapper rolled down. Primed. Half a dozen Irn Bru cans lay on their sides. Drained. Next to them in a neat pile, were several unscrunched Chunky Kit-Kat wrappers that Jimmy planned to fashion into silver goblets when he felt more energetic.

Neither Jimmy nor GI Joe exchanged a word. There was no need. One sweep of the room, one glance at the shame and self-loathing on Jimmy's face as he looked down on his stomach swelling up to meet him like a reproach, said it all.

'This you with the rest of the family?'

GI Joe picked up a framed photo from the sideboard. The only photo on display.

Jimmy, days old, lay on Aunt Pol's knee. He was asleep, mouth curled in a crescent smile as though he was harbouring some secret. No one else in the picture seemed as content. Dad's expression was grim, the way Jimmy would always remember him. Mum was anxious, frowning over Aunt Pol's shoulder as if she couldn't trust her daft wee sister to hold a wean without dropping it. Aunt Pol – nothing like her dolled-up, laid-back, twenty-first century self – held Jimmy as though he was a bomb ready to detonate. At fifteen, she looked years older than she did nowadays.

GI Joe frowned into the photograph.

Just go, Jimmy screamed silently at the top of the priest's head. *Leave me alone.*

'This Dad?' GI Joe asked.

'Yeah, he's dead. Cancer.'

'Patrick mentioned that. Tough, Jim. I'm sorry.'

Before GI Joe replaced the picture, he ran his fingernail slowly around the swaddled bundle in Aunt Pol's arms. 'Lovely wee baby,' he said, almost to himself, then turned, catching Jimmy's eye before he had the chance to look down. His voice was gruff, but more kindly.

'A wee tidy-up here then we'll get out for some air.'

It was an order, not a suggestion.

'Starving, eh, Jim?' said GI Joe, very quietly, as Jimmy clunked his giant Dairy Milk in the bin.

Not anymore, gulped Jimmy. The amount of rubbish he had scooped off the floor made him sick with panic. How? Why did he do this to himself? It never made him feel better.

Jeez, it was sweltering, much hotter outside than in. Jimmy could hardly get a breath. GI Joe strode towards the Botanic Gardens, arms straining the sleeves of his grey priest shirt as if he was heading some SAS character-building punishment mission. Jimmy lumbered alongside, the contents of his stomach sloshing and churning audibly.

'Looking a bit warm there, Jim.' GI Joe turned into the gardens and steered Jimmy to a bench beneath a shady tree, the pressure of his hand printing a sweat leaf on Jimmy's t-shirt.

'Sit!' GI Joe ordered, his command a benediction to Jimmy's ears. From a backpack, GI Joe withdrew a tatty photograph wallet. And a bottle of water.

Nectar, screamed Jimmy's thirst.

'Need help with this, Jim,' said GI Joe, passing a couple of photographs to Jimmy. Hesitating. Then passing the water casually.

Gulping water, Jimmy's eyes swept the first photograph. There was a miniature GI Joe staring back at him, dressed in a sweaty-looking vest and shorts. Spit of Bruce Willis in one of his action movies. *Diehard.* Even had his head shaved. He stood in front of some kind of hut. Low and long. Constructed from irregular strips of corrugated iron. Painted whacky colours. Roof was a tarpaulin secured by stones.

'That's my place. Way out in the bush in South Africa.'

There was no hiding the pride in GI's voice.

'I've only two rooms right now. Need to make it bigger.'

How barren the place looked. One ramshackle building and the man in front of it. In the foreground, rough soil, bare of grass. Nothing on the horizon. No trees. No houses.

And it looked hot.

'Looks like the middle of nowhere,' said Jimmy.

'Exactly what I said when I first saw it,' said GI Joe. 'Day's drive to the nearest town.'

'The middle of nowhere,' Jimmy repeated. 'Why d'you live there?'

GI Joe slid the second photograph in Jimmy's hand over the first one. Taken from the same angle, the tumbledown was still there but Jimmy could hardly see it for people. Dozens of them, mainly children of all ages, laughed and pointed at the camera. They had long brown sinewy limbs, huge glittery eyes, *huger* glittery smiles. GI Joe was in the middle of the group hunkered level with two skinny boys whose arms snaked around his neck. He was laughing too.

'That's why, Jim. That big girl there; Martha. She's bright. Needs school.

'There's Wee Joe in the Glasgow cap – I'm Big Joe. Won't speak. Dad hacked to death. Machete. Wee Joe witnessed it. That baby. Beautiful, yeah? John. Hardly cries. Dumped outside my door one night. Animal could've got him.

'Ima, with the smile. She takes care of him. They're all orphans, these kids. Most parents died of AIDS . . .'

Jimmy was happy enough to let GI Joe ramble on while he rehydrated. But he couldn't figure what a dump in the middle of nowhere had to do with him. Unless Mum had stuck his name down for the Missions behind his back.

He listened while GI Joe explained how the hut – 'falling down round our ears' – functioned as a schoolroom, dining room, church, town hall. Medical centre once a month if the doctor made it.

'I mean, look at the place. We've nothing, Jim. That's not right, is it? If you met my kids, you'd give them the moon . . .'

GI Joe wiped sweat from his forehead, thumped his fists on his knees. Clenching. Unclenching. He breathed deeply, sucking air through his nostrils as if he needed to calm down.

Chill out, man, thought Jimmy watching a congo-line of perspiration dance the vein in GI's temple.

'So you're here to raise money for charity?' He thought he'd better say something before GI's head exploded.

'No, I'm not after charity, Jim. Hate that word!' spat GI Joe, with a glare that glued Jimmy's wet back into the wood of the bench. 'Every kid, *every* kid, deserves a decent childhood. By right. Health. Education. Nutrition. Love. By right. Nothing to do with race. Nothing to do with religion. A child deserves the chance to build on the talents it's been born with, not bury them.'

GI Joe snatched his photographs, shoved them in his backpack and yomped from the park.

'Food for thought, Jim,' he hurled over his shoulder at the park gates.

What was he on about? Psycho priest. Jimmy exhaled through his teeth, mildly irritated. Dragging me all the way out here for nothing. I'll bake for him if that'll get him off my back. What else could he want *me* to do?

Inside the nearest bus shelter, Jimmy cooled his forehead against its metal wall. There was no one else waiting for a bus. Only Jimmy, and a voice in his head that wouldn't shut up.

Coach was talking about you as well as those kids, it said.

CHAPTER 7

KEEPING COOL

'You told me you'd hay fever. I come up to see the invalid and find out he's away with that dude at St Jude's. What does he want, Jim?'

'Who? GI Joe?'

The faintest flicker of a smile crossed Aunt Pol's face. 'That's what you call him?'

'He takes us for football,' Jimmy explained.

'He's signing you for Scotland?'

Jimmy shrugged. 'Wants me to bake, I think.'

'And of course, you'll say yes. Smart, Jim.'

Jimmy *was* smarting. Hated when Aunt Pol gave him grief.

'He showed me pictures. Lives out in the middle of nowhere. South Africa.'

'Looking for a cook, is he?'

'Think he wants me to do that here,' said Jimmy sheepishly. 'To raise money. He wants a new building for the kids he looks after.'

'Jim. You're a softie.'

Aunt Pol was mellowing.

'What do I keep saying? You don't have to agree to things . . .'

'. . . just because people expect you to,' Jimmy chimed.

It was one of Aunt Pol's top ten catchphrases.

And it always made her laugh when Jimmy finished it for her.

'Well,' she rapped Jimmy gently in the temples, 'practise what I preach, my son. Fancy the flicks? *Some Like It Hot.* A classic.'

The cinema was busy for such a roaster of a day. Jimmy was glad he and Aunt Pol had arrived early. They always did these days, having learned the hard way. Last time they were late Jimmy had jammed, squeezing into a row as the opening credits were rolling. Vic Swift's big sister started squealing that his bum was smothering her.

Jimmy and Aunt Pol hadn't stayed for the film that time. They left, laughter flapping behind them in waves with each swing of the door.

'Mission Impossible Three,' Jimmy joked feebly on the way home, only joking at all because Aunt Pol looked so crumpled and sad for Jimmy's sake.

Today, as the film began, and stragglers inched their way into the few remaining seats, Aunt Pol drew up suddenly beside Jimmy and inhaled sharply through her teeth.

Someone, half-crouching, had darted for a single seat in the front row.

Aunt Pol muttered something under her breath that Jimmy couldn't catch. 'Blowing in' and 'bad smell', the only words he made out.

'Whassup?' he whispered.

'Shh,' Aunt Pol answered, digging him gently in the ribs.

'That was mega,' said Jimmy.

The film had transported him to a place where he could shed his fat self. For two hours, he was just a punter like everyone else, enjoying the film. Then he stepped into the afternoon heat. It blasted his face like a shot from the blowtorch he used to caramelise his crème brûlée, sucking away the joy that had built up inside him in the darkness.

'Good, wasn't it?' said Aunt Pol fanning herself with her hand. She attempted a Marilyn Monroe wiggle along the cobbled lane which fed on to a main shopping street. Then she thought better of it. Changed direction.

'Too busy that way,' she said, 'folks exposing bits of themselves that should never see the light of day.'

Jimmy knew fine she was sparing him the gawps. Heat like this always turned him beetroot.

'What d'you like best about the film, Jim?' she asked.

Jimmy was no longer in the mood to answer. Hot and thirsty, the uneven cobblestones pressing uncomfortably into the soles of his feet gave him the gait of a grizzly.

Why couldn't he be handsome like Tony Curtis or George Clooney, funny like Jack Lemmon, Adam Sandler. Cool like Sean Penn?

Why couldn't he be someone else altogether? Normal.

'Well?' nudged Aunt Pol. 'You were laughing your head off in there.'

'End was best,' said Jimmy reluctantly, 'when the wee millionaire proposes and the other guy confesses he's a man and the millionaire says –'

'"Nobody's perfect."'

Jimmy and Aunt Pol stopped dead as a voice interrupted them.

'Classic,' interrupted GI Joe, grinning at them both.

Aunt Pol said nothing. Stood, arms folded defensively across her chest for what felt like a bad-mannered eternity to Jimmy, until GI Joe's smile faded. With an awkward cough he moved off.

'Enjoy your evening folks. Catch up with you tomorrow, Jim.'

What was that all about? thought Jimmy, watching GI Joe retreat. Nothing like a priest, he thought, in his shorts and faded Pulp t-shirt. Just a bloke. Being civil. Maybe wanting a bit of company. An image flashed into Jimmy's mind: GI crouched among the kids in the middle of nowhere.

Jimmy frowned at Aunt Pol in bewilderment.

She *never* acted like this. Downright rude. Face set as she watched GI Joe. Waiting until he'd blended in with the Saturday crowds before she moved herself. He must have been the bad smell she'd mentioned in the cinema.

'Gie us peace, Holy Joey!' she muttered after him.

'What's up with him?'

Vaguely, Aunt Pol waved her hands.

'My al-*lergy* to the cl-*ergy,*' she sing-songed.

But Jimmy knew Aunt Pol was lying. And she never lied to him.

He stared at the top of her head wishing he could see inside to her thoughts as she stirred her cappuccino in their favourite café.

In the dream that night, the top of Aunt Pol's head was platinum blonde, like Marilyn Monroe. She wouldn't look up when he called her name and pointed to the Shadow Shape.

'Aunt Pol, what's up? Tell me.'

CHAPTER 8

GI JOE KICKS ASS

'So, think the Swimathon'll be a good fundraiser, Jim?'

Jimmy was sneaking out of Mass before the end, tiptoeing as best he could down the front steps of St Jude's when GI Joe caught him. Caught him in more ways than one. Of course, Jimmy had remembered GI Joe wanted to see him. But there being no sign of him at the back of the church, Jimmy had convinced himself that GI Joe had forgotten.

Doh! Nabbed, thought Jimmy, nodding unconvincingly at the ground.

During Mass, Jimmy had been *vaguely* aware of Father Patrick's usual dronesville sermon including something about fundraising to help all our less fortunate brothers and sisters overseas. Blah. Blah. Blah.

His brain had pressed the off button at that point.

'Jim?'

GI's voice was stern, its tone accusing.

'You mean you didn't hear the sermon? I'm disappointed.'

Jimmy squirmed.

'Sorry,' he mumbled, making a futile attempt to shuffle past GI Joe. Escape was becoming a matter of urgency, not merely because GI Joe was giving him grief. People were beginning to spill out of church. Kids from school among them.

'Hey, lighten up, Jim.' GI Joe's hand circled Jimmy's elbow, shook it playfully. 'Kidding. I don't listen to that old codger, either. But come back in the church and I'll show you . . .'

This was worse, infinitely worse than any genuine rebuke from GI Joe. To be ushered through a jostling congregation, letting the very folk you wanted to avoid feast their eyes.

Mum, there's *the fat boy in third year I told you about*!

Here, thought Jimmy, was a fundraising opportunity *extraordinaire* for GI Joe. All he needed was a megaphone:

Roll up. Roll up. See Fat Boy Fat in the flesh. Pound a stare.

Jimmy raised his arm to wipe the sweat of embarrassment from his forehead, bumping Victor's mother who veered to avoid him, her mouth pursed in distaste.

Ellie McPherson, new to the school, slipped round Jimmy and away. Her hair piled up on her head looked like chocolate curls. Without her special glasses on, at least *she* wouldn't have seen him. Jimmy blushed all the same.

Finally Mum emerged with her wee wifey pals from the choir. 'Not like your Jimmy to hang about,' Treesa, their leader, bawled with as much subtlety as her singing.

Heads turned. Stared.

'He makes you look awfy wee, Father Joe,' one of the other women cackled.

'Here, we'll need to hide all the home-baking if your Jimmy's coming in for a cuppa in the hall, Maeve.'

Enough already. Jimmy wrenched his arm free of GI Joe's grip, turned and pushed his way through everyone on the church steps. Ducking his head so low that his chins compressed his throat, he headed for the bus stop but swerved away. He knew the girls standing there.

'No' coming to join us, big boy?' one jeered. Senga, Victor's squeeze. 'Plenty of you there for all of us.'

Someone else made a loud vomiting noise and another voice lisped. Chantal McGrory. 'No theatth for uth if he getth oan, Thenga.'

Jimmy walked, keeping his eyes on the pavement. As his bus passed, he heard the girls banging the window at him.

Just get home he told himself, doing his best to step up the pace.

'Oi, Jim,' he thought he heard someone call at his back. Although he didn't turn round. Kept walking until someone stepped in front of him.

Not again.

'That was rather rude back there.'

There was an edge to GI Joe's voice; he was the hard-man coach again.

'Manners cost nothing, you know.'

Jimmy shrugged, and began to move away. *Leave me alone.*

'Where you going now? I'm still talking to you, Jim.'

'Look.'

Something flashed inside Jimmy and before he could stop himself he was staring GI Joe straight in the face.

'I've said I'll bake for you, OK? Just get off my back.'

Jimmy gulped.

Never in his *life* had he stood up to anyone. He forced himself to eyeball GI Joe.

In his chest, something had come alive. It was glowing like a coal. It was warm. It felt brilliant.

GI Joe had taken a step backward, holding up his hands in a gesture of submission.

'*That's* more like it,' he rasped, eyes boring into Jimmy, challenging him to say more. Then he grinned, not in the mocking way that Jimmy was used to when anyone grinned at him, but as though the pair of them were in cahoots, sharing some secret.

Jimmy felt his cheeks grow hot, the warm coal inside cooling as suddenly as it ignited. His rush of anger fled, mind turning cotton-woolly and flustered. He looked down.

'So, Jim.' GI Joe's hands landed, paw heavy on Jimmy's shoulders. Leaning forward, he growled in

Jimmy's ear, 'You've a set of balls in there somewhere. Now we can do business together. Tell me what I can do for you.'

'Don't want anything.' *Weirdo.* Jimmy tried to shrug the hands away.

'I'm late,' he added, feebly.

'For what?' GI Joe's voice was searching. 'For hiding yourself away?'

Leave me alone.

'You're happy with things as they are? Rather I ignored you? Left you to fester like a blob in your kitchen. Left you to binge yourself into an early grave steeped in your own misery. Left your big fat arse to rot. *Gie us peace.* That's all you want. Well – I'm sorry.'

Jimmy couldn't believe what he was hearing. Responsible adults didn't speak to him like that.

Mum wouldn't even have scales in the house. She never mentioned his weight, even on Obesity Clinic days.

'We've got hospital today,' she'd say, making sure she shredded any new diet sheets the consultants gave Jimmy the minute she got home: '*How . . . are you . . . expected . . . to live . . . on this rabbit food*?'

Not even Aunt Pol, who thought Mum was too soft with the diet, ever talked about 'fat'.

'Let's get fit,' she'd say every New Year. 'A mile jog every evening. I'll stop smoking.'

But it never lasted. Bad weather and overtime, flu and homework meant that any fitness drive was over before it started.

Nobody, not even the consultants who gave Mum such a hard time, ever used the word *fat* in Jimmy's presence.

Now here was a *priest,* calling Jimmy a blob, a fat arse. Kids at school had called him less and been suspended.

'Jim, *look at me, will you*?'

GI Joe was shouting. One or two people passing glanced over their shoulder at him.

Aye, you're right. This guy is *a nutter. Help*! Jimmy wanted to call after them.

'Look at yourself, Jim. You're the saddest, most miserable sod I think I've ever come across in my life. Sadder in your own way than my wee souls in South Africa. And that's saying something.'

The paw tightened.

'Fourteen, Jim, and you're dead inside. Standing on the sidelines of your own life, miserable as sin. When you gonna change? When you gonna make things better?' GI Joe shook his head, voice quavering as he backed off Jimmy at last. Jogging away.

'I want to know how I can help you before I let you help me.'

CHAPTER 9
SUNDAY LUNCH

'Soup's great, Jim,' said Aunt Pol.

'Mmmm,' Mum agreed brightly, smacking her lips. She exchanged glances with Aunt Pol.

'Something up with it, Jim?'

Both women had let their bowls grow cold. They watched Jimmy toy with his spoon. He hadn't touched his soup. Carrot and coriander with ginger. His favourite.

'Maybe too hot for soup, Jimmy?' Mum pushed her bowl away. 'Salad would've been better.'

'Plenty of that in this house,' snapped Aunt Pol, quick as a flash. 'Deep fried lettuce.'

'That's unfair.' Mum was defensive. 'We eat greens, don't we Jimmy?'

'Not enough,' snorted Aunt Pol when Jimmy didn't

answer, and before he had the table cleared she and Mum were going hammer and tongs about what *should* be in a healthy diet.

This dispute wasn't a new one, but today there was something forced about it; Mum and Aunt Pol trying to cram noise into the silence Jimmy's mood had spun.

Jimmy was normally at his best cooking Sunday lunch, a feast that tended to last all the way to teatime. Today, no one wanted seconds and the wine Aunt Pol had brought remained unsipped. While Mum and Aunt Pol argued, Jimmy slipped off to his room.

Fat arse.

Dead inside.

Miserable as sin.

GI Joe's words churned like ingredients boiling in a stewpot. They burned. They hurt. Gnawed Jimmy like hunger.

Reaching under his bed, he withdrew his stash of emergency rations. Unwrapped a multipack of Mars bars, settled back on the bed. Its frame creaked, springs twanging a tone poem of warnings under Jimmy's backside as he swung his legs up with a grunt and nestled against his pillow.

His mouth filled with soft sweet flavours: toffee, mallow, creamy milk chocolate. They coated his teeth and his tongue, plastering the arch of his palate. Jimmy allowed himself a little sigh.

That's better, he told himself. You needed that.

Stop it. Look what you're doing to yourself, a voice in his head implored.

Jimmy unwrapped another Mars bar. Noisily. Stuffed it whole into his mouth making loud mashing noises, pulping the chocolate. Chomping down so he wouldn't hear his nagging voice of reason:

Stop. You're making yourself ill. You have to stop.

I've had a rotten day, Jimmy justified himself.

He'd finished the packet. Fifteen Mars bars journeying through his digestive system. Jimmy lay back and pressed his belly. His hands disappeared into a squish of flesh. He moved them upwards to his chest. He shuddered, crossing his arms over his shoulders, cupping the spot that GI Joe had gripped so earnestly.

His fault, that psycho priest. If GI Joe hadn't said all

those things, Jimmy would never have skelped those Mars bars. Now he was feeling worse than ever.

I want to know how I can help you, GI Joe had said. Tough one that, thought Jimmy. Let's see: Can you find me some mates?

Can you whisk me away and set me up in my own restaurant far, far from here? Where the only things I'll worry about are choosing ingredients, blending flavours, inventing sauces, cooking . . .

When he closed his eyes, Jimmy could see himself, clad in the checked trousers and stacked white hat of a chef. He stood in the middle of a stainless steel kitchen. Around him winked gleaming pots and pans. Ranked before him was an armoury of utensils essential to the working chef.

In his mind's eye, Jimmy opened a swing door into his well-stocked pantry. On shelves, tidy rows of ceramic jars stood to attention, labelled in his own handwriting:

CORNFLOUR CUMIN CURRY POWDER

Tins on the floor. Bulky dried goods on the first shelf.

Fragrance of basmati rice tempered by the tang of dried herbs. Jimmy knew the layout of his pantry better than the stretch marks on his belly.

SUGAR

He reached for the sugar jar without needing to look for it . . .

But his hands clutched air. And the pantry doors swung closed behind him. There was no smell of dried food in his nostrils.

Only chlorine.

Jimmy was back at the swimming pool of his dream.

There was Aunt Pol, waving anxiously from the gallery. She was jabbing her finger towards the deep end. Jimmy scrunched his eyes, tried to see what she was on about. He could only make out a blurred shadow in the distance.

'What?'

He shouted at Aunt Pol in frustration.

'Who is it? Tell me.'

Then he had a brainwave. Eureka! Why did he have

to swim to the end of the pool when he could walk around its perimeter?

He moved off, still in his chequered chef's trousers. One step, two steps. Excitement beating a pulse in his throat. At last, the answer to his dream quest: Shadow Shape, who are you?

He took another step, foot raised in mid-air, ready to surge forwards.

'Jim. What are you doing to yourself, man? Stop. You'll drown.'

GI Joe's features, slick on the head of a seal, emerged from the water millimetres from Jimmy's foot. He blew through the ref's whistle in his mouth as he spoke.

'Stop.'

The pool had widened, completely filling Jimmy's dreamscape. Any pathway to the deep end of the pool had vanished. There was only one way for Jimmy to reach his Shadow Shape.

'Go and get changed,' said GI Joe. 'I'll help you swim.'

CHAPTER 10

TOUGH LOVE

Jimmy didn't feel he'd been asleep, but must have been. His mouth was thick with the aftertaste of too much chocolate. There were great ridges down one side of his face where he'd lain on crumpled wrappers. His hair was plastered to his forehead with sweat.

He felt awful. Heavier than ever staggering into the hall, bulk compressing his lungs, denying him breath in this airless afternoon.

He leaned his head on the cool wood outside the kitchen, wheezing. On the other side of the door, Mum was shouting:

'– you think Jimmy should be out gallivanting, do you? Meeting girls? You of all people. You've a short memory, Pauline. A very short memory.'

There was a long, long pause. Something hanging, thought Jimmy. Unsaid.

'It's not the same for Jimmy, and you know that.' When Aunt Pol spoke, her voice was minute. 'I just wish he was – you know, *normal.* I mean – he's pathetic. Bingeing because he's so flipping miserable. No pals. What existence is that for a teenager?'

'I hope you're not suggesting it's *my* fault –' Mum's voice quavered in indignation.

'– You *know* I'm not saying that,' Aunt Pol interrupted. 'I know what you've done. And I'm grateful. It's just – I look at Jimmy, and it cracks me up inside. He's enormous, and we're letting him get that way.'

Jimmy winced at what came next:

'Our Jim's fat. Obese.'

'He is *not.*'

'Gross.'

'He is NOT!'

'And he's getting worse. Where did I put that article?'

Jimmy heard objects clattering on the table as Aunt Pol tipped her handbag out.

Pathetic, Aunt Pol had just called him. *Fat. Obese.*

How could she? Aunt Pol. Who never seemed to notice his size. Jimmy didn't even feel fat around her.

'Here it is. Fat Farm. Somewhere in Yorkshire. You get the GP to refer him –'

Mum's voice quaked as she cut in. 'Why are you saying this, Pauline? Jimmy's fine here. He's going nowhere. I watch his diet.'

'Ach, you never make him stick to anything. Buy him junk. Let him comfort eat. You're too soft. Jim needs tough love.' Aunt Pol sighed then added so quietly that Jimmy had to strain his ears. 'You should know.'

'Pauline.'

There was silence. Jimmy could hear the kitchen clock ticking on the mantlepiece. A chair scraped.

'Sorry,' whispered Aunt Pol.

She was crying. Aunt Pol, who never, ever cried. 'He breaks my heart,' she said.

Not since Victor, Maddo and Dog-Breath chased Jimmy with knives and forks, chanting *Kill the Pig* had Jimmy moved so fast.

The knowledge that Aunt Pol thought the same

things about him as everyone else twisted Jimmy's stomach like a dose of indigestion after a dodgy pudding supper. It hurt.

CHAPTER 11

HELP

Out in the street, Jimmy felt vulnerable. Exposed. Everyone second-glanced him: from the bloke lovingly waxing his car, whose bonnet darkened with Jimmy's passing reflection and who turned to gawp at the real thing, to the old dear sitting in her deck chair lost in the *Sunday Post.* She lowered her reading glasses, stared and stared until Jimmy was out of sight.

'Get a load of that, Darren,' Jimmy heard a man tell his son as they suspended a garden kick-around.

'Who ate all the pies, eh, Da?'

I'm fat, not deaf.

Miserable as he'd ever been, Jimmmy walked on. He didn't even know where he was going, having walked blindly from his row of tenements into a nearby housing scheme, taking unfamiliar side streets and crescents. Only the occasional flash of an orange bus hurtling along the main road assured him he wouldn't get completely lost.

Crikey, was Jimmy bushed walking! Heart going like the clappers, t-shirt stuck to his back. He was breathless. Parched. Would never make it home on foot. Fumbling among the sweetie papers in his pockets for change he made for the main road.

'Jim! Isn't it too good to be inside this weather? I was gonna come and see you later. Now we can walk and talk.'

GI Joe, in his Bruce Willis get-up, bounded from nowhere like a supercharged pit-bull. Gave Jimmy's shoulder the old paw clamp, steered him away from the stop, as a bus – Jimmy's bus – hurtled past.

'Guess what, Jim?'

'What?' Jimmy's voice was as heavy as his heart. *That was my bus* he wanted to say. Instead, he found himself lurching alongside GI Joe: Frankenstein's monster without the neck bolts.

'It's brilliant! I've got the Leisure Centre for a whole

day and night the month after next. Gonna run that Swimathon right enough and have a big party after. Music, dancing. What d'you think, Jim? Fancy running the catering side for me?'

Jimmy just about managed a grunt of agreement, although he didn't see how he could look ahead to next month on this, the longest walk. He didn't think he'd even make it to the next block! Deep within the flesh of his thighs, which chaffed, sweaty-raw against each other, untried muscles quivered in spasm. Every few steps, one or other of his legs jerked a warning: *I can't go on.* If both legs jerked simultaneously, Jimmy would drop like a very large boulder on the pavement.

His nostrils, possibly the fittest part of his anatomy after his jaw, worked overtime to suck oxygen into his lungs. A pointless exercise. The more Jimmy inhaled, the more exhausted he became. His fingertips tingled and his head buzzed as though it was going to burst from the strain of matching GI Joe's walking pace.

He was dizzy.

Felt sick.

Had a stitch.

Was knackered.

But still they walked, and GI Joe talked. Yak, yak, yak. All the way home.

Only when Jimmy sank on the steps of his close did GI Joe zip it. Arms folded across his chest, legs astride, he stared, watching the sweat run from Jimmy's pores. Down his arms, over his heaving chest, through his hair.

'Look at you, man,' GI Joe said at last.

He hunkered down, bringing himself eye-level with Jimmy. Grabbed the back of his neck. Shook him like a dog.

'What you doing to yourself, man?'

Those words were *déjà vu,* thought Jimmy. Dream words.

'That was only a couple of miles we walked, Jim. What a state you're in. I'll help you.'

Hadn't he said those very words in the dream? The swimming pool dream where the Shadow Shape lay forever out of reach . . .

'C'mon, Jim. Tell me how I can help you.'

Of his own accord, Jimmy met GI Joe's gaze. What if . . .? he was thinking as he blinked sweat from his eyes. And aloud he whispered the rest of what he was thinking.

'. . . you could teach me to swim?'

'Where were you, Jimmy?'

Two worried faces peered through the steam of the bathroom watching Jimmy emerge wrapped in an enormous bath sheet; a corpulent Roman emperor.

'Pauline said Father Joseph brought you home.' Mum took Jimmy's elbow in her hand, cradled it as if he might break. 'I went out looking everywhere, son. Are you all right?'

Over Mum's shoulder, Aunt Pol was frowning deeply at Jimmy.

'Why were you with that priest again?' Aunt Pol said 'priest' as though it tasted foul.

Jimmy took his time answering, looking from one face to another. Mum's cheeks were tight, and pale. She was just glad that Jimmy was back and safe. No more questions. But Aunt Pol, she was acting well weird, looking at Jimmy through narrowed eyes as though he'd done something wrong.

'Went for a walk,' he shrugged. 'I'm going to have some of that soup now.'

'And you just *bumped* into St Action Man by chance.'

'Pauline!' whispered Mum.

'Something like that,' said Jimmy.

The women crowded him at the cooker.

'Something like what? What's he been saying?' Aunt Pol practically spat the words out. It wasn't like Jimmy to play games, even mind games.

'He's gonna teach me to swim. Says I've got swimmer's shoulders.'

'What?' Aunt Pol's tone made Jimmy glance up from the soup he was stirring. He frowned.

She had turned whiter than a slab of buffalo mozzarella.

MAIN COURSES

CHAPTER 12

I DON'T LIKE MONDAYS

Two minutes to nine.

He was going to be late.

Jimmy stumbled from the bus – already pulling off while one leg was still on – and groaned.

He should have taken a chance. Alighted with the other kids from St Jude's. Who knows? Monday morning. Folk might not have been in slagging mode yet.

Now Jimmy would join the Latecomer's Line outside the Heedie's office. The Usual Suspects in the line up would tease him as per:

Jumbo Jimmy Fifty Bellies.

Piggy in a blazer.

Everyone passing the Heedie's door would gawp as though Jimmy was on temporary loan from the

Museum of the Revolting. Cheeky wee first years doing impressions to amuse their mates, puffing out their cheeks and chests, holding their breath until they turned beetroot, waddling from side to side, belly-bumping anyone coming the other way up the corridor.

Why was he late today? Not today. All the classes in third year were having an assessment first period to sort out English sets for next term. If Jimmy made the top set he'd have Mrs Hughes again next term, a fantastic teacher. To give himself a fighting chance he'd had an early night to make sure he didn't sleep in. And he'd actually had a great sleep. No bad dream last night. No Hungry Hole this morning. But now the day was going downhill even though it was uphill all the way to St Jude's. A steep, steady rise. Jimmy's legs felt stiff, jerky. He pecked. Heard the bell ring.

How tempting, how very tempting for him to about turn and retreat into the peace and comfort of his own bedroom.

Mum wouldn't mind. *Quite right to come home, son. Shouldn't overexert yourself.*

No!

The hand of responsibility settled in the small of Jimmy's back and pushed him onwards.

'No!' Jimmy swore he heard a real-life female voice echo. Jimmy froze.

Up ahead, in the bin alley by the school gates, several girls formed a tight huddle.

Jimmy's blood ran cold as he homed in on the scorpion ankle tattoo and platinum perm of Senga McGuiness.

'Beam me up, Scotty,' he implored.

Last time this coven had pressed him up against a wall, Senga had made Chantal unbutton Jimmy's trousers to see if he wore a corset. Too late. He'd been clocked. Chantal McGrory already nudging Senga.

Jimmy shuffled onwards, bracing his shoulders against the first attack.

'Ith it twinth ow twiplets?' Chantal lisped. Senga, the ringleader, seemed otherwise engaged. She had someone trapped in the middle of the huddle.

'I said *no*! Leave me alone,' cried the same voice Jimmy had heard a moment ago. This time he recognised it.

'*Leave me alone*,' Senga repeated in a wheedling

voice. 'Posh, in't she? Gonny make me?' she added with a snarl.

With a flick of her wrist, Senga sent Ellie McPherson's spectacles skiting along the ground. They landed near Jimmy's feet.

'Stop it. I *need* them.'

'I need them,' voices cackled back, as Senga lunged for the spectacles, one foot raised to smash them.

And at that moment, two remarkable things happened.

First, Jimmy beat Senga to the quarry, bending with a grunt to snatch Ellie's specs before Senga's trainer squished them. Second, from the deepest recesses of Jimmy's chest, a voice yelled:

'Leave her alone.'

Jimmy launched himself at the two henchgirls who held the struggling Ellie in their grip. They were so taken aback when Jimmy butted in that they let Ellie's arms go and she plunged like a missile from a catapult head first into Jimmy's chest.

'Would you look at the state of they two,' Senga cawed as she and the coven linked arms and moved away.

'She's blind and he's desperate. They were made for each other.'

'Y'awright?'

Jimmy couldn't see where Ellie was because he didn't dare look up, and she couldn't see because she just couldn't see, so they both stabbed blindly in mid-air until their fingers jabbed into each other and Ellie took her glasses. At her touch even Jimmy's fingers blushed.

'Thanks.'

Speechless, Jimmy waved Ellie and her thanks away.

But he stayed put in the bin alley. Needed a few moments. To collect himself. Things were happening in his body. Started happening when Ellie McPherson headbutted him in the chest; intensified when she touched his fingers. Made him feel well weird, but didn't hurt. Made him want to punch the air, sing out the first line of all his favourite songs, and at the same time stick his head down a hole so no one could see how luminously he was blushing.

How Jimmy made it from the bin shelter to the Latecomer's Line, he couldn't tell. Maybe angels pushed him there on castors. He certainly felt as if he was floating, even when the Heedie wheeched him out the line by the tie and tugged him all the way up the English corridor to Mrs Hughes' room, waving a detention slip in his face like a matador baiting a bull: 'Move it, for once in your life, Kelly!'

For the first time in a long time, Jimmy didn't care. Didn't care what he looked like lumbering after the Heedie. Didn't give a toss that the sight of him had reduced the Usual Suspects to a hysterical heap outside the Heedie's door.

Ellie McPherson. The sooner he reached his English class, the sooner he'd see her again. That was all that mattered.

CHAPTER 13
TEN YEARS ON

Ten Years On

Mrs Hughes wrote on the blackboard.

'Think about it,' she said, in that quiet voice of hers, her eyes scanning everyone in the room. Even Jimmy looked up. You had to, if you wanted to hear what Mrs Hughes was saying, because she wouldn't repeat herself, and she wouldn't shout.

'You'll all be ancient. Twenty-four. Twenty-five. Some of you parents. Yes, maybe even you, Alistair, God help us.' She smiled, leaning close – but not too close – to Dog Breath Doig.

'Some of you'll know what they want to do with their lives already, but others'll have given their future no thought. That's fine.'

Mrs Hughes spoke even more quietly. Jimmy's ears strained to catch her words.

'So before you begin this assignment, I want you to shut your eyes. Come on, Victor, I'm the only one who'll know if you don't look cool. Imagine you're wearing virtual reality helmets and they pitch you forward ten years. What do you see in your future? What are you doing? Matthew, since you haven't bothered closing your eyes, maybe you can tell us what *you'll* be doing ten years on.'

Maddo, creasing double at his own wit, announced, 'Ten years, Miss. Geddit? Ah'll be dain' ten years.'

'Fiona?' Mrs Hughes cut into the wave of admiring sniggers before Maddo threw in one of his prison stories.

'I'll be modellin', getting' intae a bit of actin'. Oh, aye, an' livin' in London. Away from this dump of a city.'

'Ambitious, Fiona,' said Mrs Hughes, diplomatically. 'You're muttering something, Victor. Spit it out.' Mrs Hughes plucked the rubber that Victor was about to fire at the back of Fiona's head from the top of his drawn-back ruler.

Victor had a few tough choices to make. Would he

swim butterfly for Scotland or would he be a premier league footballer? 'Lot of people are interested in me,' he said leaning back in his chair, and giving himself a couple of congratulatory pats on the chest. Then he winked at Mrs Hughes. 'And I think I've got the looks to get into the music business, an' all. A kinda Pop Idol, but no' gay.'

'Just like that,' said Mrs Hughes, her mouth twitching. She moved on to Dog Breath Doig.

'Dental hygienist, Miss. Yon lassie who scrapes m' teeth every month gets to listen to Clyde One all day. That'll do me. Oh, and ah'm gonny be married wi' at least four weans.'

'Any takers?' asked a deadpan Mrs Hughes. She moved on.

'What about you, Jimmy?' she asked.

'Kelly?' snorted Victor.

'He'll have burst, Miss.'

'Cardiac arrest.'

'Look at the stupit smile oan him.'

'Dreamin' he's working in a cake shop.'

'Want me to wake him up, Miss?'

*

Ten years on I will have my own restaurant.

Jim's

My name will be up in black and gold.

Jim's

People will see it from a distance and say,
'There it is. We've found it.'
It won't be in Glasgow. Or in any city.
It will be by the sea. People will have to make a
special journey just to find it.
I might have a couple of rooms upstairs so people can
stay if they've travelled a long way.
I'll do lunch and dinner five nights a week.
Nothing too fancy.
Not too many choices.
People will know about me. Television folk will come
to eat at Jim's and they'll try to persuade me to do
a series or write a cookbook.
'Maybe,' I'll tell them.
I'll bake, too. Bread, scones, pastries. The things
people like best.

And tablet, of course.
Everyone gets a bit of that. Even if they come in for a coffee.
At Christmas, I'll make loads and put it in fancy boxes.

Ten years on, I'll have my own restaurant.

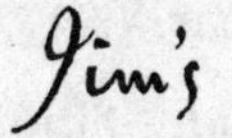

And I won't be this size any more.

'Ten years on, Jimmy, where will we find you?'

'In the Guiness Book of Records.'

'Stuck inside his house wi' his maw running after him because he's too big to get oot.'

'Doing nuthin', fat loser,' concluded Victor, as Maddo banged his desk-lid to jerk Jimmy out of his reverie.

Mrs Hughes silenced the growing ripple of insults with a frosty finger.

'Jimmy?'

No way was he going to curdle his dream in front of this lot. Especially when Ellie McPherson was turning, trying to focus on where he was sitting. He wasn't daft.

He dropped his head so that the faces jeering at him disappeared.

'Probably working in an office,' he shrugged. The first, the least controversial, thing he could think of.

'Ellie?' Mrs Hughes smiled at Jimmy: *Well done for saying something.*

Ellie's voice rang clear.

'Travelling,' she said. 'Finding lots of out-of-the-way places.'

Hope you find Jim's, wished Jimmy, slatting his eyes open just enough to see the back of Ellie's chocolate brown hair through his lashes.

'Finished at last?'

Mrs Hughes smiled at Jimmy when he handed over his essay, and bumped his way out the classroom, thighs knocking against all the desks.

'Must be some office job, Mr Kelly.'

Ellie was now the only pupil still writing, her face practically touching her paper, hair tumbling over the sides of her desk. Jimmy hovered inside the classroom door, willing Ellie to hand in her essay and join him. He had to content himself with a half-smile from her as Mrs Hughes shooed him outside. It was halfway through morning interval and the corridors were thronged.

Jimmy, head full of Ellie sitting at a table in Jim's, stepped out of the classroom without planning ahead, and was immediately swept along towards the one place he did not want to go: the lower-school bogs.

'Well, well. Look who's no' got his catheter in the day?'

Maddo, on sentry duty at the bog door, denied two wee first years entry with a knee to their bladders, but caught Jimmy by the arm and wheeched him inside before he could escape to the playground. 'Stand back everyone, Pavarotti needs a wiss.'

Wedging the toilet door shut with one boot, so no one else could come in, Maddo shoved the other against Jimmy's buttocks. The force knocked Jimmy off balance. He stumbled, falling hard on his hands and knees. At Victor's feet.

'Fag?'

Victor held the soggy end of his cigarette to Jimmy's

mouth, pushing it roughly against his clenched lips.

'Why you down beggin' if you don't want it, you fat toad,' he said as Jimmy jerked his face away.

The toe of Victor's boot caught Jimmy under the chin. Forced his head back until he could see Maddo's face grinning upside down behind him. Then with a flick kick Victor sent Jimmy sprawling backwards on to the dirty toilet floor.

Through cigarette fug Jimmy looked up at the sneering faces of Victor, Maddo and Dog Breath. Beached and helpless, he was surrounded. He prayed that Victor had forgotten what he did the last time he had Jimmy in the toilets, sticking his head down the pan just after Maddo had been in. But before he'd flushed.

'New blazer, Jimmy?'

Victor's tone was deceptively friendly as he knelt down beside Jimmy's head and flicked ash on to Jimmy's face and collar.

'That was daft, leaving the other one in the shower, you plonker. Oops.' Victor wet his finger with spit and rubbed ash into Jimmy's lapel.

'Kelly's blazer looks smart the day, eh? No' a mark

on it.'

As if on cue, a shower of ash rained from three cigarettes while Jimmy struggled to raise himself to his elbows.

'Goin' somewhere?' Dog Breath pinned Jimmy back to the ground with his foot. Then he cleared his throat and let a thick, green grog slither through his lips. It landed – splat – on the edge of Jimmy's sleeve, and dribbled on his hand.

Even Victor groaned.

'Ye manky prat.'

'Well, what we gonny dae wi' him now?' asked Dog Breath impatiently, aiming a slow-motion practice kick at Jimmy's head. 'Let's gie'm a doin'. This is borin'.'

As Maddo lunged forwards, Jimmy was saved by the interval bell.

Dozens of boys, clutching their genitals, stormed the bog entrance and dived for the urinals. In the mêlée, Jimmy picked himself up. He locked himself in a cubicle dusting ash and muck from his blazer as he waited for the place to empty. His hands were shaking. What would Ellie think of her rescuer now, if she saw the jelly state of him? She'd surely be as disgusted with him as he was with himself. A miserable sod. With a lurch Jimmy recalled the priest's words. GI Joe was right. He should never have wasted his time getting the blazer dry-cleaned in the first place. Nothing was ever going to change for Jimmy.

When he thought the coast was clear, Jimmy slipped the bolt and tiptoed into the corridor.

'To be continued, lardy arse,' hissed Victor in his ear, smacking Jimmy across the top of the head as he swaggered ahead of him.

CHAPTER 14
REFUGEES AND CHOCOLATE ECLAIRS

'Why have I got you in my class this period?' Busty Bacon asked, blocking the doorway to her room. The formidable bosoms which had given rise to her nickname were trained on Jimmy like two giant Toblerones.

It was the first lesson after the toilet incident. Should have been music, which Jimmy loved. Would have cheered him up after all that grief from Victor. Hamblin, however, had hijacked this period to run end of term team games for anyone who was interested. Jimmy wasn't and, fortunately, as he discovered when he turned up at the PE block, neither was Hamblin.

'Wheeze your way back to the office, Kelly, and find someone with room for one more this period.'

The school secretary sent him to Busty's room. She didn't want him either: 'Is this a joke, James Kelly? Physical education offloading you to domestic science?'

Busty rolled the words 'domestic science' around her mouth as though they tasted far too fancy for the likes of Jimmy, and sniffed up one nostril.

'No, miss, I'm here,' Jimmy mumbled at the floor.

Busty, clicking her tongue in vexation, ushered Jimmy into the classroom as her pal, Mrs Dunlop – The Tyre – St Jude's other domestic science teacher, passed with her knitting.

'Get the coffee on, Gina,' Busty called lightly making a drinking gesture with her pinkie crooked as though she was a toff. 'Give me five minutes to get my refugees sorted. I've two now,' she sighed, as though the class size was too much for her, 'and one of them,' she went on, her voice swelling to a boom as she closed the door on The Tyre, 'thinks she can waltz into *my* classroom with her manky, dirty hair down! Here. You. Eleanor McPherson.'

Quickly waving Jimmy – whose ability to breath, let alone move, had deserted him at the mere mention of

Ellie's name – to a worktable, Busty plucked an elastic band from her wrist and flicked it dismissively across the classroom towards Ellie. Jimmy watched Ellie reach out to snatch it and miss. She had turned to watch Jimmy's entrance instead. At the smile Ellie gave him, his legs buckled slightly as he edged into the same row where the elastic band had landed.

'I can see why PE can spare you, dear,' Busty snapped impatiently.

'Ellie.' Jimmy's cheeks burned as he said her name for the first time, stretching across his cookery table. He was holding out the elastic band in his fingers, but Ellie couldn't see what he was doing. She was too busy looking for the band on her own table, her hair pooling the surface.

'Filthy! Hair!' said Busty, marching up behind Ellie, seizing a spatula on the way. Keeping Ellie at arms length, mouth pursed, Busty reached for her hair and raised as much of it as she could gather on her spatula. Jimmy thought she'd have been happier lifting a dog turd by the look on her face.

'Quick, you,' Busty's fingers clicked at Jimmy for the

band, but he didn't move. How could he, when he was watching warm chocolate ripple over the spatula?

Wow.

Ellie had amazing hair. Good enough to eat. Thick. Dark. Brown. Naturally kinky. And heavy. Jimmy noticed how Busty's arm drooped under the weight of the hank she held out on the spatula.

Best of all were the cloudy coils that sat on the surface of Ellie's hair. They glowed in the sun. Caramel golden. Transparent.

Only once could Jimmy remember seeing a colour like that. Aunt Pol had taken him to see a celebrity chef make magic with molten sugar, spinning it into brittle spirals that glistened like the finest golden thread.

'Gee yourself, Kelly. Pass that band.' Busty's voice and fingers snapped Jimmy from his daydream.

He felt his own eyes water as Busty snatched the elastic, yanking Ellie's head back at the same time. Ellie winced as Busty stuffed her hair into an unruly ponytail.

'Much better.'

Busty scoured her hands with pink carbolic, smiling over her shoulder.

'If that hair's not tied back next time, dear, I'll cut it off. Got it?'

'Yes, miss.'

Ellie's voice sounded as tiny as her face looked with her hair drawn back, thought Jimmy. Her exposed cheeks blazed as hot as Jimmy's felt in her presence. Without realising it, he had moved from his own worktable to stand next to her.

'Would you look at the pair of you lined up like rotten eggs. There's a recipe on the board. Éclairs. Cream in the fridge. Don't lick the chocolate when you melt it – you listening, Kelly? Bring a plate of your best ones along to the base for Mrs Dunlop and I to mark. And –' she was halfway out of the door, '– no malarky. Clear?'

'Yes, miss.' Ellie's voice was barely a whisper.

'Sorry?' More of the bosom appeared in the doorway.

'Yes, miss,' Ellie spoke up.

'Better, dear. Next time, try to look at me when I speak to you.'

There was silence in the huge cookery room. Jimmy could hear Busty stump off on her ridiculous stilettos to the domestic science base.

Wait for me, miss, a terrified voice bleated inside him. This was, after all, the best and the worst moment of his entire life so far. He was alone with Ellie, but he didn't have a clue what to do next.

Luckily, Ellie broke the silence.

'She should have said "Mrs Dunlop and me".'

'What?'

'Busty said "Mrs Dunlop and I". Bad grammar. Silly cow.'

Ellie, half-standing, slid herself and her stool along the worktable and plonked right next to Jimmy. A coil of her hair tumbled loose from her elastic band and bungeed up and down beside her ear like a mischevious spring.

'I can't cook,' Ellie groaned, breaking the silence again. And again.

'Can you?'

Jeez. She'd asked Jimmy a direct question. He would have to answer. Rude not to. Jimmy felt himself blush. Ellie was so close. She wasn't looking at him, however.

Ellie's eyes went all funny if she didn't wear her glasses. And she tended not to wear her glasses. Her pupils drifted about, each doing their own thing. They never actually crossed, just bobbed gently and wouldn't focus. Jimmy liked that. It gave her a faraway, kooky look.

Maybe that was another reason why Ellie made Jimmy feel funny. He could look at her and she wouldn't know he was watching.

Skellie Ellie everyone called her. Then Speccy Malecky when she put her glasses on. A lose-lose situation.

'Busty gave you a hard time.'

Where did that come from? That was twice today Jimmy had spoken around Ellie before he could swallow the words back.

'Y'all right? And after this morning with Senga?'

Ellie nodded vaguely in Jimmy's direction with a dreamy smile. She was trying to blow away another spring of hair that had loosened from her ponytail.

'Did she hurt you when she pulled your hair?'

Jimmy thought there was something different about his voice – although it was still his own voice. It sounded deeper, older.

Not only that, his legs seemed to have their own

agenda. They were side-slipping closer to Ellie while he spoke.

Move any nearer and he'd be able to brush that curl away from her forehead.

He gulped.

Too close. What did he think he was doing?

Back off, you big balloon, before she pushes you off, he warned himself. No one likes your fat in their face.

'Hurt me?'

Jimmy couldn't believe it. Ellie stood up and stepped towards *him*. And then she smiled. At *him*. Big, full-on friendly smile.

'Nah!'

Ellie was standing up proudly. She stepped even closer to Jimmy and screwed up her eyes so she could see him better.

She was still smiling as she tugged her hair free and let it tumble over her shoulders. Still smiling while she nibbled at the elastic band until it broke, her eyes dancing with mischief.

'Ooops. Silly me.'

She dropped the band daintily on the floor, where it lay, twisted like an anaemic worm.

That's when Jimmy had the brainwave.

'Chocolate éclairs,' said Jimmy. 'I'll give Busty chocolate éclairs.' For being so mean to the tastiest girl in the world, he thought, setting out flour, butter, bowl.

'I can't cook, I told you.'

Ellie moved closer. She tried to see round Jimmy's bulk and her hair touched his shoulder. A jolt from a friendly cattle-prod.

Crikey!

Jimmy had to turn away and get a box of eggs from the fridge. He knew his face was scarlet. Not that Ellie could see – although she *must* have *heard* the eggs rattling against each other in his love-shaky hand.

'You dead short-sighted then?'

Jimmy had to say something. Any closer and Ellie would land on top of him.

'Mmmmm,' Ellie said dismissively as though it didn't matter. 'I see bright things. Like the colour of your hair.'

It wasn't an insult. Jimmy looked Ellie in one

dancing eye at a time just to make sure. No spite there. No malice.

Ellie groaned again. 'I've never followed a recipe.'

'Me neither.'

Jimmy sifted flour into a bowl, raising his sieve really high so that flour particles fell like the lightest snowflakes.

'Busty's got the amounts wrong anyway. If I use all the butter she says these'll never puff up right.'

'You've done this before?'

Ellie was so close she practically bumped the sieve from Jimmy's hand. The length of her arm touched his own, but she didn't pull it away like anyone else would do. Her touch made Jimmy shivery then hot inside, like he'd gulped from a mug of cocoa on a cold, cold day.

'I'm no help here,' Ellie groaned again, watching Jimmy cut butter into tiny squares and drop them into boiling water. 'I was looking forward to music, not domestic science.'

'Me too,' said Jimmy, swallowing the urge to ask her if she liked the same singers and bands as he did. That would have been pushing his luck way further than it had gone already. Just keep her by your side like this a wee bit longer, he cautioned himself. 'Whip this cream,' he told Ellie, 'I'll do the rest.'

They were perfect.

Twelve ginormous oblongs straining the sides of the baking tray.

'Wow! They're twice as big as when you put them in.'

Ellie had put her glasses on to whip the cream, so at least she could see something despite the white flecks spattering her lenses and the great dollop of chocolate sauce that Jimmy's finger itched to wipe off her nose.

'I mean they're all exactly the same size. And none of them are burnt. They're golden. And the smell – buttery, and floury, and *oooh*!'

Ellie sniffed the tray like a dog exploring new territory. She was going on the same way about Jimmy's baking as Aunt Pol, he realised, although similar praise from Aunt Pol never gave him jelly-baby legs like this.

Jimmy told Ellie to pick out the four best éclairs,

holding out a plate so that he could watch her profile while she concentrated.

She had millions of freckles, not great big chocolate button ones like he did. Ellie's were dots like cinnamon dust on cappucino.

He sighed inwardly.

'So these are for Busty?'

The éclairs Ellie had chosen crammed the plate.

'No! These are.' Deliberately, Jimmy tipped what remained on the baking tray to the floor.

Then, with a bit of a grunt, Jimmy plonked to his knees. He took an éclair in each hand, and ever so gently, careful not to damage the pastry, rolled them across the floor, back and forth, making sure they touched Ellie's elastic band.

Next, he ran the éclairs under the lip of the cooker just far enough in to collect any gunge that may be lurking there. He trailed them along the bottom of the cookery bench until he came to a corner. There lurked a dustball, studded with crumbs and hairs and what might have been a leaf but could have been anything from someone's shoe.

'Your turn,' said Jimmy to Ellie. 'You finish the others the same way, and I'll do the cream and chocolate.'

'Then we'll take them along –'

'– to the base,' giggled Ellie, attempting a Busty teeter.

She hunkered down facing Jimmy, her face so close that he could have flicked out his tongue like a lizard and licked the chocolate off her nose.

'You're brilliant,' she whispered, looking straight at him, her one good eye magnified behind its thick lens. There were green bits among the hazel. The colour of mint cracknel.

So're you. Desire nudged Jimmy's larnx. Say something, you big wumman's blouse.

'Got chocolate on your nose,' said Jimmy, flicking it off with his finger. Irresistible.

The first, the lightest touch.

He scrambled to his feet, praying Ellie couldn't hear the thumping din from the depths of his ribcage. **Baboom**. **Baboom**. **Baboom**.

'Come on,' he said to drown the noise. 'Can't keep Busty waiting.'

*

'AB-SO-*loot*-ely *DEE*-licious, James Kelly. Beginner's luck,' said Busty, calling from the window of The Tyre's car as it drove out the playground. 'Tell that wee McPherson girl she's a born cook.'

'*Fab*ulous!' The Tyre chipped in. 'Mrs Bacon ate three!' She pointed at her passenger who, to Jimmy's delight, was looking a bit green around the gills.

Result! thought Jimmy, marrying the teachers' compliments to the portrait of Ellie hanging in the gallery of his heart.

There was actually a spring in Jimmy's lumber as he passed the pitch on his way out of school. He imagined himself walking over lightly-toasted marshmallows; just firm on the surface yet squashy underneath. It was such a pleasant sensation that Jimmy almost delayed dropping his head when he realised that the figure doing star jumps, while GI Joe prowled a circle around him growling, 'Faster, *faster* if you wanna be a pro,' was Victor.

Jimmy definitely didn't want Victor to see him. Slag

him. Spoil a perfect day. Well, perfect in the end.

Nothing should stop the cream of this day floating to the surface of his mind.

Not only had he managed to bake undercover in school. Instead of doing gym.

But he'd made a friend.

And she was gorgeous.

'AB-SO-*loot*-ely *DEE*-licious!' Jimmy couldn't help whispering to himself once he was home. He was making Ellie a mini-disc, because it turned out she liked nearly all the same music as he did, wondering if the Ronettes 'Be My Baby' (Aunt Pol's all-time favourite song) was a bit too obvious. He had settled instead on Aretha doing 'Respect' when the phone rang.

'*Ree-ah-ree-ah-ree-ah-ree-ah-ree.* Just a little bit . . .' Jimmy hollered into the receiver, expecting Aunt Pol to sing back to him, but there was silence when he stopped holding the receiver like a mike and put it to his ear.

'Jim?'

It wasn't Aunt Pol. It was GI Joe. Deadpan.

'Poolside. Seven. No armbands.'

Jimmy had completely forgotten.

CHAPTER 15

'TO BE CONTINUED', CONTINUED

Heat smacked Jimmy like a wall in the face as the swing doors opened into wet changing. Every noise was amplified. Music throbbing so loudly over the PA system that the tune was unrecognisable. Its beat made the floor vibrate under Jimmy's feet. Babies cried in relay behind cubicle doors and from the pool itself, frenzied shrieking rose and echoed to the rafters over the splash splash splash of water.

Chlorine and shampoo and sweat and nappies assailed Jimmy's nostrils as he plodded across the scummy floor to the changing cubicles.

A woman stared, nudging her daughter as Jimmy, unable to fit sideways into a single cubicle, reversed out again.

She was still staring when Jimmy took a vacant family cubicle. As he locked the door both woman and daughter exploded with laughter outside.

If there had been a mirror in the cubicle Jimmy would never, ever have ventured outside in the luminous orange, lotus-patterned XXX-large shorts Mum's pal Treesa had brought Jimmy back from Hawaii two years ago. The label was still on them. They were too long and at least one size too tight, the waistband bisecting the swell of Jimmy's stomach.

'Cheery,' Treesa had described them.

Criminal, more like, Jimmy had thought as he thanked her enthusiastically at the time. I'll never be seen dead in these.

Steeling himself, Jimmy bundled up his clothes and crept from the cubicle to the lockers. With the rubber band that held his locker key disappearing into a cushion of flesh at his wrist, Jimmy looked nervously towards the pool.

He hesitated, resting his damp forehead against the cool metal of the locker door. Could always say he turned up and GI Joe wasn't there.

Could say the heat of the place bothered his asthma. Could say –

'Well whaddya know. It's the pig in curtains.'

Jimmy froze. Squeezing his eyes shut. Pressing his forehead harder against the locker door in the hope that he might pass through it by osmosis.

'What you doin' here, lardy boy?' Maddo snarled, slapping Jimmy round to face him. Victor, behind Maddo, said nothing. Flushed, breathless, his sleek racing trunks already wet, he peeled his squad swimming cap from his head, sucking greedily from a sipping bottle. Opening a locker in the same row as Jimmy's he threw in his cap, float, leg brick. All the time looking Jimmy up and down, up and down, from head to toe, assimilating every square millimetre of what he saw. His eyes lingered particularly long on the shorts; a thin, mean smile on his face.

'You're late, fat boy. Squad training's over.'

'Gunna empty the pool, are you?' grunted Dog Breath Doig, face so close to Jimmy that there was no escaping his horrendous halitosis.

Maddo knuckled Jimmy in the solar plexus, the pain

forcing him to wince and straighten up to his full height.

'Vic's talking to you, blubber-belly,' Maddo hissed.

'I . . . I'm getting a lesson.'

As one, the three boys closed in. 'You're no' seriously showing yourself in public?' said Victor, voice low and dangerous. He was wearing fancy goggles around his neck like an extra pair of eyes. 'We canny let you do that,' piped Maddo who, like Dog Breath, was changed for swimming. Jimmy reeled back from the sour sweat smell of Maddo's armpit combined with Dog Breath's dog breath, as with sudden force Victor slammed Jimmy against the lockers, piercing his shoulder blades with two protruding locker keys.

'Ugh,' Victor shoved Jimmy again, revolted at having touched the film of sweat covering Jimmy's entire body.

'You're disgustin'.' He stepped back, whipping Jimmy's towel from under his arm.

With a flick he snapped the towel open, catching Jimmy hard on the cheek before he could flinch.

'Fat-disgustin'-loser.'

'Fat-disgustin'-loser.' Maddo and Dog Breath

automatically joined in the chant as Victor flicked the towel again. This time it glanced the side of Jimmy's eye, drawing tears.

'He's greetin'. The blubber's blubbering.' Maddo guffawed as Jimmy curled instinctively, clutching his eye, leaving his back exposed to the next swipe of his towel.

They were all prancing around him now, in a mad dance. Skinny white bodies and bare feet. Maddo and Dog Breath poking Jimmy's belly, slapping his backside, chucking his cheeks and making quick karate kicks at his legs while Victor drew the towel back for another swipe and another swipe. Welts rose over Jimmy's torso as he swayed helplessly out of the firing line while Victor choreographed his moves to the relentless, concealing throb of the poolside music.

'This – *flick* – would be a lot more – *flick flick* – fun if you – *flick* – fought back, you fat poof,' said Victor, throwing in the towel at last. At last he made to drop the towel into the filthy wet gully that gathered slops from the changing areas.

But that was when GI Joe lunged from a changing

cubicle right next to the lockers in time to catch Jimmy's towel before it hit the ground.

'A word, gents,' he said shepherding Victor, Maddo and Dog Breath out of sight, leaving Jimmy slumped against the cool metal of the locker doors, his towel pressed hard against his eyes.

CHAPTER 16

TAKING THE PLUNGE

'They're a shower of wasters, Jim,' said GI Joe through clenched teeth when he returned to Jimmy. 'You're bigger than the lot of them put together when they behave like that. Now. Let's do this.'

Meekly, Jimmy followed GI Joe down the row of lockers to the poolside.

He felt wobbly after Victor's assault. Drained. Close to tears. Last thing in the world he wanted to do now was make another fool attempt at swimming. He'd never be like Victor in the water, needing all that impressive squad paraphernalia. Why on earth had he asked GI Joe to teach him swimming? Jimmy and water just didn't mix.

How long had GI Joe been in there, anyway, Jimmy

wondered? And why hadn't he come out sooner? Why wait until Victor and his sidekicks were getting tore in before he intervened?

This wasn't the time to ask. GI Joe was already at the shallow end, jerking his head impatiently for Jimmy to join him. Here was a moment Jimmy wished more than anything that he could be invisible.

No such luck.

There might as well have been an announcement over the PA system:

EYES LEFT EVERYBODY –
FAT BOY ON THE MOVE

because any head that wasn't underwater turned to get an eyeful.

There was total hiatus in the pitch and thrum of the pool, all eyes following Jimmy as he lumbered into view behind GI Joe. Silence echoed through the sticky, chlorinated air.

The pool's surface smoothed to a millpond as swimmers froze.

Even the music stopped.

Then reaction began to ripple across the pool. There was laughter. There were sharp intakes of breath. There were kids pretending to make tidal waves.

Jimmy shrivelled. Shrunk inside. Died a thousand deaths. But there was no escape.

'Jim, pay attention.'

GI Joe didn't mess about. He positioned Jimmy at the shallow end of the pool, shuffling him forward until his toes were over the edge. Jimmy had to trust him. After all, he couldn't see his own feet.

'Step forward,' GI Joe barked as though he were on a parade ground.

'Don't look down and you'll land in the water standing up. It'll be over your waist, but you'll be fine.'

GI Joe's hands gripped Jimmy's upper arms.

'Don't push me,' Jimmy wheedled before he could stop himself, cursing his fear.

'Don't PUSH me!'

Last time Jimmy had been near a pool; the one and only school swimming lesson the PE department would let Jimmy take, he'd uttered these same words. Victor had been at his back, mimicking: *'Don't PUSH me!'* About to dunt Jimmy into the pool where the water would come over his chin. Nearly choking him. Hissing words in Jimmy's ear that sent him off balance even before he was pushed.

'See your Auntie. My mum says she's no' really your auntie –'

Jimmy was twisted round, mouthing a puzzled 'Wha –?' at Victor before he was felled.

'Timb*errrr.*'

'Don't push me.'

'I won't,' said GI Joe, releasing his grip on Jimmy's arms. 'You'll do this all yourself.'

Plumbline-straight Jimmy fell, feet touching the bottom of the pool much, much sooner than he would have believed. The water reached no further than his waist. Just as GI Joe had promised. He'd done it.

From the corner of his eye, Jimmy watched Victor watching him. Keenly. Eyes narrowed. Arms folded. He stood shin deep in the kiddies splash pool ignoring

Maddo and Dog Breath who lay on their backs before him frothing the water with their feet. He turned away slowly, as GI Joe slipped into the water beside Jimmy and with the sides of his fists, thumped Jimmy at the top of each shoulder. Coach was grinning from ear to ear.

'That took guts, Jim,' he said. 'Well done.'

CHAPTER 17
SWIMMING

All that hassle, thought Jimmy, drifting off to sleep, and we didn't even do any swimming. GI Joe wanted to leave that until the morning. 'Seven thirty, when this place opens.'

He'd made Jimmy kneel until only his head was above water. For one cringing moment, Jimmy feared he was going to get a blessing. But no danger. Coach just wanted Jimmy to hold his breath and sink s-l-o-w-l-y under the water breathing out, and then come up again s-l-o-w-l-y, still breathing. Made him do it about fifty times, and after Jimmy became used to the sensation of the water over his head and round his face, it was a doddle. He felt like a twat at first, right enough, but once Treesa's trunks were underwater, people ignored him.

Only Victor noised him up, repeatedly diving above him like a low-flying jet. Victor's dives, long and streamlined – beautiful – flew him in an arc nearly a third of the way up the pool before his body cut the water. It would be another third of the pool later before he surfaced, ploughing to the deep end with one, two, three sleek strokes of front crawl.

'Waster. Tries hard when it suits him,' muttered GI Joe. Like Jimmy, he watched Victor give the finger to the pool attendant pointing out the NO DIVING notice.

Several dives later, Victor was marched from the pool area by two attendants. 'Looks like you're having a ball there, Coach,' Jimmy heard him say to GI Joe with a chummy click of his tongue as he swaggered towards the showers. 'Away you home and grow up,' GI Joe replied, turning away from Victor back to Jimmy.

But Victor didn't go home. Strange, thought Jimmy, breaking through the water for the umpteenth time. Once changed, Victor sat alone in the spectators' gallery, arms draped over the safety rail, frowning as he watched Jimmy with GI Joe.

When the lesson was over and Jimmy heaved

himself up the pool steps, he sensed something other than Victor's mockery in the eyes boring his wet torso and tracking his journey to the cubicles. It felt more like resentment.

Victor was in Jimmy's dream tonight too, sitting where Aunt Pol usually sat. He wouldn't budge when she arrived and asked him to give up his place. Instead, Victor pointed towards the deep end. Jabbed at the Shadow Shape. Whispering in Aunt Pol's ear, eyes smirking all the time at Jimmy. But Jimmy couldn't hear anything that was said because the music in the swimming pool dream was too loud. 'Heroes', his favourite Bowie track, blasted through his head on a loop.

GI Joe was standing over him in the shallow end wearing Jimmy's hideous Hawaiian trunks. They were so big that GI Joe had cut arm holes in them and wore them as a baggy costume. Jimmy felt sorry for him, dressed like that. He felt relieved that he wore proper racing trunks like Victor's now. And goggles. A real swimmer.

Trapped in dream paralysis, Jimmy watched as Victor leapt from the spectators' gallery and dived expertly over Jimmy's head. One dive propelled him all the way to the deep end, landing him just where the Shadow Shape hovered. His body, as he waved smugly back towards Jimmy, obliterated the Shadow Shape completely.

'Wait,' Jimmy's dream voice called, body aching to push off from the side and reach for the deep end. He stretched out both arms, kicking off against the side of the pool with all his strength.

And he flew, cutting the water like a torpedo. Whoosh, whoosh whoosh. Ellie, a mermaid, wearing her specs instead of goggles, passed him underwater, hair floating around her head in a giant halo. She was blowing him bubble kisses.

In fast-forward, Jimmy passed Dad – who ignored him – in the armchair. He dodged kicks from Maddo and Dog Breath, circling him like sharks after meat. Ducked squares of tablet Father Patrick flicked at his head as he swam by.

Jimmy strained for the deep end. For the first time

ever in all the years of his swimming pool dream, he could make out the tiles marked:

DEEP END
DEPTH 2 METRES

He was going to meet the Shadow Shape at last.

Blood pounded his ears from the effort he was making. His lungs were bursting as, with one final lunge, Jimmy reached for the edge of the pool.

Was that a hand there? Fingers reaching towards him? Ready to pull him out? Ready to greet him?

Jimmy arms strained their sockets, stretching for tantalising dream fingers. He lifted up his head, gulping in air as he surfaced. He opened his eyes, groping the darkness of his bedroom for the hand of the Shadow Shape. And –

CRASH!

toppled to the floor with a humungous thump.

CHAPTER 18

WEIGHTLESS

Jimmy couldn't help it. Kept floating off all through English.

Whole body rising up out of the seat, hovering horizontal over the class. Like Superman.

What a feeling!

If only he could pluck Ellie from her chair. Tuck her in the crook of his arm, pointing his fist at the open window. Together they would fly out, off to enjoy a day exploring the stratosphere.

Up, up and awayyyyyy!

Late night supper on Krypton; coffee and tablet. Then home.

Jimmy was celebrating.

He could swim.

Three hours ago he had learned to swim. Nothing had ever felt so good.

Two lengths.

Skoosh-case.

Look! *I can swim everybody*, he shouted silently at the class. And it was all thanks to Ellie. Not that she knew that.

Jimmy had made such a clatter falling out of bed that the downstairs neighbours thumped their ceiling with a stick. That had woken Mum. When she saw the state of Jimmy – a big, dazed, sweaty, breathless heap on the carpet – she nearly had the emergency doctor out.

Refused point blank to let Jimmy go to school: 'School? You're going in an oxygen tent, never mind school.'

No school, thought Jimmy, would mean no more Ellie until fourth year, and the thought of that hurt more than the purple bruise on his shoulder sustained when he tumbled out of bed and landed on his inhaler.

So he kept his appointment with GI Joe. Lied to

Mum to do it. Told her they were discussing the Swimathon catering budget in the school gym.

'Ouch!'

GI Joe had greeted Jimmy with a friendly punch on that sore shoulder. The pain reactivated last night's dream, flashed up the highlights:

Victor watching through narrowed eyes.

GI Joe in that outfit.

Ellie, the kissing mermaid.

Jimmy losing the Shadow Shape. Again.

GI Joe threw Jimmy some goggles and a pair of big dusty brown trunks. 'Wakey, wakey, Jim. Try these for size. Can't have you showing me up in wallpaper today,' he said.

The trunks smelt of tobacco and damp. The elastic around the waist was perished. Jimmy didn't like to ask where they came from, in case GI Joe confirmed his suspicion: they'd crawled from Father Patrick's underwear drawer.

The pool was eerily quiet, stretching awake for the new day. Jimmy had his pick of the changing cubicles. The floors were clean. No music played, so the only sound was the rhythmic, soothing thrash thrash thrash of early morning swimmers – heads down, caps on – putting in their lap-fix before breakfast.

When he analysed it later, staring at the back of Ellie's head during English, trying to figure how many different shades of brown he could distinguish, Jimmy realised he *knew* he would swim today.

Last night's dream had primed him. Trained him up. Had left him with the *nearliness* of reaching the Shadow Shape.

At such an early hour, the spectators' gallery was dark, no one, especially no Victor, looking on. Judging. Criticising. Mocking. Even the pool attendants – who had watched Jimmy nervously last night – were ignoring him, swabbing the poolside like sleepwalkers.

'Do what you did yesterday,' called GI Joe. 'Put your face in the water and count to three. Then surface. This time though . . .'

. . . you've got to lie horizontally, like in the dream. An inner voice whispered through a secret earpiece in Jimmy's head. *Remember you pushed off from the side and stretched your arms out in front and you flew –?*

'. . . imagine you're Superman, Jim. You won't sink. Look I'll show you.'

Jimmy twitched, impatient, as GI Joe waded alongside him and demonstrated what he wanted Jimmy to do. Legs against the side. Arms out. Face in the water. Kick off and –

Fly. You'll fly, Jim. Try one stroke.

Jimmy didn't need anyone to show him. He already knew.

Suddenly, like a light switching on inside him, he realised the ability to swim was there. Always was. Stored under layers of blubber and misery.

In the DNA.

Buried deep.

A secret.

That first stroke was the hardest. Not immediately, when the initial push-off carried Jimmy away from the side and out into the pool. That felt magic! Jimmy was weightless. Flying. Swimming. Then that momentum faded, and Jimmy began to sink towards the bottom of the pool. *Game over. Wheech him out with the big hoop and call the paramedics.*

Not today. Not after last night.

Through his goggles Jimmy could see GI Joe's hands in the water ready to grab him. Ready to help him stand. Say, 'Not bad, Jim. Let's try it again.'

Not today. Not after last night.

Because Jimmy wasn't ready to let his weight suck him to the bottom.

So he kicked. Not gracefully, but not disgracefully either. It was an instinctive frog-kick, strong enough to lift his legs into the horizontal position and keep him afloat. And so he kicked again, and again, and before he knew it, he was well past GI Joe. Kicking. Floating. Breathing. Swimming. All the way to the deep end.

His lungs were bursting as he grabbed the side, and hauled his head out of the water.

'Yesss,' he spluttered, imagining the Shadow Shape's long fingers reaching down, shaking his hand.

CHAPTER 19

SOOKS

'Ten years on? Who knows where I'll be, or what I'll be doing. Maybe I don't want to write down too much in case that limits me. After all, the world's my oyster.'

Mrs Hughes surveyed the class over her reading glasses, and sighed. 'Now that,' she said, 'had vision. Excellent!'

'Who done it, miss?'

Maddo's eyes slid suspiciously over the class.

'Don't worry, Matthew, it wasn't you.'

Under cover of snorting Victor muttered, 'That Skellie Sook,' just loud enough to attract a glare from Mrs Hughes.

'With a couple of exceptions, most of these essays were *extremely* disappointing,' she went on over the dying laughter, fixing her eyes on Victor. 'In style, *and* content. Most of you think you'll be picked out to join some band who don't write their own songs, and writhe around semi-naked on children's television.'

'Sounds a' right to me,' snuffled Dog Breath.

Mrs Hughes sighed. 'Pack up, you nosey lot.'

Blink and you'd miss the imperceptible glance of approval that Mrs Hughes sent to the back of the class where Jimmy sat. Unless you were Victor. Paying attention when it *really* mattered.

'Sook,' Victor snarled under his breath, grinning like a hungry shark who's just spotted lunch on the horizon.

'Jimmy. Excellent. Well done.'

Mrs Hughes followed Jimmy out of the classroom. Behind the camouflage of his bulk, she rested the flat of her hand against his back.

'You know that when people write down their goals they tend to achieve them. You stick in there. 'Bout time we saw what you were made of.'

In the corridor, Jimmy dodged Victor and moved to catch up with Ellie. Camouflaged by the interval throng he figured he could get away with being seen beside her. He needed to give her the mini-disc he'd made.

Well: that was the pretext. He really just needed to see her. Talk to her. Get closer. Breathe in the same air she breathed out.

There she was, up ahead, tight in the middle of an arm cleek with Senga and Chantal. Totally out of place flanked by that pair, Jimmy realised, watching the trio slam quickly through the interval seethe. Ellie, Jimmy sensed, was in trouble again, although there was no way he could reach her fast through the broil of bodies clogging the corridor.

Which is why he boomed, **'Ellie!'** at the top of his voice, surprising himself even more than the scores of pupils who clamped their hands to their ears and dived aside like deafened skittles as he bowled the length of the corridor in her wake.

Not realising at first, in his haste, that Victor and co. were following in his slipstream, hustling him into the same empty classroom where Senga had yanked Ellie.

With a nod from Victor, Billy McIndope stood edgie at the door.

'Well, well, well,' said Victor, driving his knuckles into Jimmy's stomach to push him towards Ellie. 'The happy couple: Skellie Sook and Squashy Sook.'

'Pure saddos, in't they, Swifty?' said Senga, who always called Victor 'Swifty' despite his periodic promises to punch her lights out if she didn't quit.

Senga fluttered her short pale lashes, wobbling her head from side to side as though the screws on her neck had worked loose. Victor glared at Senga, driving his fingers deeper into Jimmy's belly with jerks of his wrist.

'Two stupit, ugly sooks, trying to get in wi' the teachers. Writing sooky stories, and *this* one,' Victor pistoned his arm deep into Jimmy's stomach, 'hanging about wi' *my* Coach in the swimmin' pool. What's that all about, Sook? Trainin' for the Fatty Olympics? Or –' he licked his lips, '– following the family tradition?'

'What?' Jimmy straightened up, confused. What was Victor on about?

'Yeh, what's that all about, Sook?' Maddo echoed, while Dog Breath, let rip a full-on halitosis guffaw in Jimmy's face.

'Speak.'

Victor's voice turned ugly.

'Aye, speak,' chorused Senga. She manoeuvred one sovereign-ringed hand into Jimmy's belly alongside Victor's, her other hand tugging Ellie roughly by the hair.

'So hungry you swallowed your tongue, fat boy?' asked Victor withdrawing his arm. He unbuttoned his shirt cuff, rolled one sleeve to the elbow and flexed his hand. Surgically, thought Jimmy. When Victor flashed a humourless 'watch this' grin at Maddo, who stood grinding his fist into the palm of his hand in anticipation of violence, Jimmy noticed that the pupils of Victor's pale blue eyes were dilated with excitement.

Victor's voice was a whisper in Jimmy's ear.

'Why does Coach want you to swim?' he coaxed, drawing his fist back in line with Jimmy's face. 'You better talk fast.'

In that chink of time between Victor's question and his fist descending, several things seemed to happen.

First of all, Jimmy realised that because he was only concerned about Ellie, he wasn't at all afraid of Victor. So he answered him. Calmly. 'Coach doesn't want me to swim,' he said. '*I* want to swim –'

'What for?' Victor had the question out while Jimmy was still speaking. Fist poised, Victor was frowning. Same way, Jimmy noticed, as he'd been frowning while he watched him from the spectators' gallery.

The second thing happened while Victor finished speaking. Ellie broke Senga's grasp of her hair with a karate chop that reverse-stamped the scrolled VICTOR from Senga's identity bracelet into the flesh of her wrist. Ellie meanwhile flew at Victor's upraised arm, snatching blindly – literally blindly, since Senga was wearing her glasses upside down – for Victor's fist. Her clumsy intervention was *just* enough to take Victor's mind from his target and give Jimmy a nanosecond to step aside so that Victor landed his punch, not into Jimmy's yielding flesh, but onto a hard school desk.

And that's when all hell broke loose.

Victor howled like a cowardly wolf, showing his hand to his cronies, keeping his own head averted.

'Is it cut? Is it cut? Feels like its broke.'

'Wee bit cut, Vic,' said Maddo, licking his chops at

the blood pouring from Victor's spliced knuckle.

'See what you Skellic cow's did to ma Swifty?' Senga screeched like a hoarse banshee, freezing Chantal, who, entwined with Billy McIndope, was trying to sneak away.

'Never mind Skellie. Ah'm bleedin' here,' Victor moaned.

'Need stitches on that, man,' said Dog Breath. He leaned over Victor who recoiled and moaned even louder, wafting away Dog Breath's concern with his uninjured hand.

'You're dead meat, hen,' hissed Senga jabbling a knuckle-dustered digit at Ellie, but from a distance. Her free hand clutched her karate-chopped wrist. 'What'll ah dae wi' her, Swifty?'

'*Ah* don't know, stupit,' Victor bawled into Senga's face, splattering her blouse with his blood as he waved her back. He'd turned pale, Jimmy thought, greeny pale. Shilpit. Scared. Still scared. *More* scared than he'd looked moments ago when Jimmy had answered his question about swimming.

Funny that, thought Jimmy, pushing Victor aside to

retrieve Ellie's glasses from Senga's head.

'Ouch. You'll need stitches in that right enough,' he said, peering at Victor's knuckle with casual interest. Then, with a nod to Ellie, he opened the classroom door and let her out before him as the bell rang for the end of interval.

'Are you all right?' Jimmy made sure he ushered Ellie into an alcove of the nearest quiet corridor before either of them had time to speak.

'Are you all right?' Nodding, she echoed him. For a moment, her hand reached out and rested on his sleeve. 'Thanks,' she said.

'No, you thanks,' said Jimmy. 'Think your karate chop saved me a knuckle sandwich.'

'Couldn't let that vomit Victor hit you,' Ellie sighed, slumping against the tiled wall of the alcove. She closed her eyes. 'Wouldn't it be great if we could just stay here for the rest of the afternoon in peace?'

Magic, thought Jimmy, savouring the smiling crescent of Ellie's long lashes while she wasn't looking.

'I've got physics though,' Ellie groaned, pushing

herself off the wall.

'I've got history.' Jimmy handed Ellie her glasses, but he didn't let go of them until he added, 'then I'm going swimming. I've just learned. I had to tell someone.'

'Brilliant!' Ellie was being swept along the corridor by a rush of latecomers. 'Tell me all about it later.'

This is a final announcement. The centre will close in fifteen minutes.
Would all remaining swimmers please leave the pool.

It wasn't the bing-bong chime vibrating from the tannoy, but the click into darkness as the pool lights were switched off that snapped Jimmy back into real time.

After all that hassle with Victor today he'd been so desperate for a swim he'd lied to Mum. Again. Father Joseph wanted another fundraising meeting he'd said, then slipped out with his togs hidden up his sweatshirt.

Once he started swimming he didn't have a Scooby about time, or how far he'd swum having lost count at forty – *forty* – lengths.

Smooth, strong, steady breaststroke.

Cutting the water, like the giant albino whale he'd watched on a nature programme once. This huge blubbery mass had moved with incredible grace and speed around the tank which imprisoned it, casting its dark shadow.

Until the lights went out, Jimmy had watched the progress of his own dark shadow sliding gracefully along the pool floor beneath him. The sight amazed him. Arms outstretched, he skimmed the glide of every stoke without effort, powered by stored energy in a kick that he would never have believed he possessed.

And he sensed, as he swam, that the Shadow Shape of his dreams was near, watching over him at the deep end of the pool. Daft, he knew he was, to fancy that some formless concoction of his imagination supervised his stroke. Ridiculous. But the notion galvanised Jimmy. Made him want to swim each length better than the one before. Had him surfacing every time he reached the deep end just in case the Shadow Shape was really real . . . was really there . . .

Afterwards, despite a long cool shower, sweat oozed

from every pore on the massive surface area of Jimmy's skin. When he tried to pull his t-shirt on, it jammed around his neck: TOO HOT. NO ENTRY.

Jimmy chuckled, working his giant underpants over his hips.

He'd been sweaty plenty of times: hot, sticky, and uncomfortable doing nothing more than breathing in and out of two lungs all day. But never like this.

This was a different sweat. It went with his accelerated heart-beat, and his need for a long cool drink. It went with the fire in his cheeks and the pleasant weariness suffusing his muscles.

It went with exercise.

A rivulet of perspiration ran from source in the pores of Jimmy's neck and tricked all the way down his back. It refreshed the memory of GI Joe shaking him there, like a dog, at the end of that nightmare walk in the heat.

Still chuckling, Jimmy forced his t-shirt on and left the cubicle.

'So we were having a fundraising meeting, were we?'

Arms folded, GI Joe watched Jimmy squidge through

the turnstile in the Leisure Centre reception.

Coach seemed well annoyed. His face was mottled red and purple. His eyes were bloodshot, all the skin around them puffed up as though he'd been crying. Like Jimmy, fresh sweat darkened the neck of his t-shirt.

'*"Oh, Jimmy's meeting you in St Jude's, Father."* God forgive you, my son.' GI Joe wagged a stern finger. Then he punched Jimmy in the shoulder. And grinned. 'I've been up in the gym. It looks over the pool.'

They set off walking home together. Thankfully, thought Jimmy, at a more civilised pace than last time. He was happy to enjoy the cooling evening air, letting GI Joe discuss his plans for the 'do' he was organising after the Swimathon.

There was no mention of Jimmy's swimming progress until they stopped at the street corner where they would part company.

'I'll have to show you front crawl,' said GI Joe.

'OK,' shrugged Jimmy, already walking away.

'And I'd better get you some decent togs to wear for the Swimathon.'

'What? No way! I'm only doing the cooking!'

Jimmy was too slow, of course, GI Joe having jinked round the corner and disappeared, his parting shot ringing in Jimmy's ears.

'What about getting your Aunt Pol down to see you? She can be your first sponsor.'

CHAPTER 20
SUMMER RAIN

Typical Glasgow.

End of term. Summer holidays starting at noon and it's chucking it.

Under grey skies and plastic-bag rain-mates, bedraggled pupils overtook Jimmy, squelching uphill for a last morning of school.

The usual comments pelted him.

'Need a push, Fatty?'

'Walk any slower and you'll be going backwards.'

'Too many fish suppers last night for the big man.'

Jimmy couldn't care less. Ellie was ahead and Jimmy was only interested in catching her before she turned into the girls' entrance.

He knew that the muscles in his thighs were on

go-slow. But not because of the bulk they supported. They were simply worn out after the work they'd put in last night. Thirty lengths with a kick float before GI Joe would show him the arm technique for front crawl.

And as for fish suppers. Jimmy couldn't look at one this weather. All the exercise, which Jimmy thought would have had him stuffing his face, was having the opposite effect on him.

Since he'd started swimming three weeks ago, he was eating less, not more. He had porridge for breakfast, and instead of having chips-with-everything school dinners, he made himself a big packed lunch: tuna salad sandwiches, chunks of cheese, fruit and chocolate. Ate it *al fresco* in the yard. Sharing. With Ellie.

In the evenings, if he was swimming, Jimmy ate a bowl of his soup, some crusty bread, or maybe a pasta. No pudding. Where in the past Jimmy used to gorge from teatime till bedtime, working himself easy through a multi-pack of crisps and several litres of fizz, eyes on the telly, finger on the remote, it was only water he felt like at night now. Maybe a banana when he came in from the pool.

This morning, he'd have sworn he didn't need to suck in his tum quite so hard when he pulled on his trousers.

'Ellie!'

However, he still wheezed a bit as he called Ellie's name. Wheezed some more when she stopped, and danced her funny eyes all over him, waiting until he caught up with her. His peak-flow diminished by her smile.

I think I'm losing weight. I've been swimming every day this week. You were wave-watching with me in a dream last night. You let me kiss you.

Despite Jimmy willing his larynx to work, he was struck mute as soon as he reached Ellie's side. She was so petite. He towered over her, marvelling at how the dampness in the rain had sent chocolate curls springing all over the surface of her hair. He smelt the freshness of her shampoo . . .

Take her brolly, you dumpling. Hold it over you both, Jimmy's courting self-counselled.

'Rotten day.' The best he could do. Pathetic!

Jimmy didn't even think it *was* a rotten day. The rain

had freshened the air, it was easier to breath. And that scent rising up from the moisture-parched pavements –

'Oooh, I love days like this,' said Ellie. 'Summer rain smells amazing, and sounds completely different from winter rain. It whispers down like it really shouldn't be falling at this time of year. D'you know what I mean?'

Course Jimmy knew what Ellie meant! She'd plucked the very thoughts right out of his own head.

The next thing she said sounded even better.

'You know those CDs I borrowed?' she said. 'I've run out of blanks for copying. Can I keep them a bit longer and get them back to you next week?'

Out of school.

He'd have to see her out of school.

Get her phone number.

Arrange to meet her.

Make a date, in other words.

Too many delicious possibilities rampaged through Jimmy's head. He tilted his face to the rain, letting it cool his ardour.

Some of the water must have softened his brain, diluting his wit. Instead of ignoring the voice which growled, 'Oi, Kelly,' after he waved Ellie into the girls' entrance, he ambled into the bin-lane to see who was calling him.

'See what you done?'

Here was one way to slam Jimmy back to the real world.

A spell of absence following the desk-punching incident hadn't improved Victor any. His mug was meaner than ever under his floppy blond hair as he backed Jimmy against a suppurating wheelie bin, waving his injured hand, bulbous in a filthy crepe bandage, under Jimmy's nose.

'Twelve stitches and a cracked knuckle.'

Yesssss, a voice hissed triumphantly in Jimmy's head.

'I've missed all my football sessions with Coach and it's two weeks afore I can swim with the squad,' Victor intoned. He was deadly serious. Paced back and forth in front of Jimmy. 'Why d'you have to do this? I'm racing butterfly in the Swimathon.'

'But I didn't touch you, Victor,' Jimmy sighed as the morning bell rang through the rain. He'd his last ever domestic-science-instead-of-games lesson with Ellie first period and he *had* to share it with her.

Maybe that was one reason why Jimmy couldn't feel his heart pulsing its usual bossa nova rhythm at the imminent prospect of being Victor's punchbag or pincushion: It was otherwise engaged. Or maybe it was because, Jimmy decided, Victor wasn't being his usual menacing self. He felt there was something changed about Victor's agenda. He was alone for a start, no Maddo lurking as lookout, and on his own Victor actually looked much smaller; scrawny. Inches shorter than the Vic Swift who swaggered around St Jude's with his mates as if he owned the place, getting in everybody's face. If anything, Victor was prowling in ever increasing semicircles *away* from Jimmy.

Easy, easy for Jimmy to walk away.

Which is what he did. Just walked. And Victor let him go. Didn't spit on him. Didn't give a mouthful. Merely called something after Jimmy, and the way his words came out – this was the really odd thing – it sounded as if *he* was the one being threatened. Not the other way around.

'My maw went to school wi' your *auntie,*' Victor

sneered. 'Says you'll be swimming to try an' copy your big-shot dad but,' he added, 'I tell you Kelly, I'll always be a better swimmer than you, even with a gubbed hand.'

'. . . and I don't know what Victor was on about. My dad couldn't swim,' Jimmy was whispering to Ellie as they laid out their equipment in domestic science. 'When I asked what the heck he was saying, he yelled, "Ask your auntie".'

'He's jealous,' hissed Ellie, stuffing her hair into a bobble before Busty Bacon descended, opening and closing a pair of scissors. 'You said he's been watching you swimming? Must think you're catching up on him. A threat.'

'Cut the cackle you two and get busy with that fairy cake recipe on the board. I'm in an important meeting with Mrs Dunlop for the rest of the period,' said Busty sweeping from the cookery room. 'McPherson, make sure I get samples of your work. Kelly, don't be licking the icing off the spoon. McGrory, I hope none of those veruccas that keep you off games touch my ingredients.'

McGrory was Chantal, a forlorn figure without Senga and her mates around her. Fingering the toilet paper necklace she wore to hide Billy McIndope's lovebites, she stared miserably at the lumpy mess of cake mixture in her bowl.

'No Senga today, Chantal?' Ellie asked her.

'She thaid she'd be here but she'th dogging an' ah canny dae thith rethipe,' Chantal whined, shrinking her head into her neck like a tortoise going into hibernation when Jimmy came round to see what she was up to. She was squirming Jimmy realised, left alone with the very pair she tormented non-stop, no brazen pals for back-up. But he didn't turn the tables as he could have done. Although he whisked her bowl away. Stared into it. Then scraped its contents into the bin. Rinsed it out.

'We can't do this recipe either, Chantal,' he said cheerfully, giving the bowl back. 'Stand beside Ellie and copy me.'

'Thenga'th no talkin' to me the now because I wouldn't dog it today,' said Chantal, lisping spit into her cake mixture. 'She'th goin' up the woods wi' Victor because it'th Maddo'th last day at Thaint Jude'th and they're all gonny get wathted. Ah'm no intae that; neither'th Billy.'

'The secret's in the beating,' interrupted Jimmy, wishing Chantal would put a sock in her mouth. Talk of Victor and Maddo, the very suggestion of Dog Breath's dog breath, let alone the thought of Chantal and Billy McIndope sucking the faces off each other, was putting him off. It was hard enough to explain in words a skill that came so naturally to Jimmy, without having some glaiket doolally lassie breathing her chewing gummy, nicotine breath all over him.

'You only need half the butter in Busty's recipe. Then crack your eggs in – thank you,' said Jimmy, as Ellie obliged with a salute. 'Chuck in your sugar. And flour. No. *Self-raising,* Chantal. This is a sponge mix, remember. And beat, and beat, and beat. Don't bother creaming everything separately like Busty says, either. Here.'

Jimmy handed the electric whisk to Chantal. She wouldn't have the wit to talk and operate an appliance at the same time. He kept one eye on her while he helped Ellie with the seemingly complex task of arranging paper cases on a baking tray.

The two of them kept sneaking smiles at each other, so they didn't see where they were putting the cake cases and their fingers would collide. Each time Jimmy made contact with Ellie, a sweet shock jolted all the way up his arm to the roots of his hair, via his heart.

'Nothing fairy about them is there?' said Jimmy, depressing the top of one golden sponge cake. Like his éclairs, his fairy cakes had risen to humungous size, and emerged from the oven shouldering each other for space on the baking tray.

'Thought youth couldnae bake?' gasped Chantal in amazement.

'Hey, Jimmy, what about some organic icing to finish them off?' Ellie grinned at Jimmy and squirted saliva through her teeth.

'Grog flavour, you mean?' Jimmy stroked his chin thoughtfully. 'What d'you think, Chantal?' he asked, dead serious, '*Essence de Phlegm*?'

'Naw, we canny,' said Chantal, horrified, fingering her toilet paper bandage as Jimmy seived icing sugar into a bowl. 'Youz are dithguthtin.'

'Only joking, Chantal,' said Ellie, smiling at Jimmy. 'Sooks like us would never do anything like that.'

'Here, Chantal.' Jimmy placed two freshly-iced cakes into her hands as the bell rang. 'Once for you and one for Billy.'

'Give you energy,' laughed Ellie, nudging Jimmy, 'When you're bloodletting.'

CHAPTER 21
BUTTERFLIES AND MERMAIDS

Jimmy could feel his face scarlet.

Not from embarrassment, but from effort.

How many lengths was it now? Felt like hundreds that GI Joe had had him wiggling up and down the pool, arms outstretched, holding a float, while his legs learned the new stroke. Butterfly.

It was only when Jimmy surfaced to take a breather and felt the blood surging around his face that he realised how hard he was working. The actual *rhythm* of the stroke itself, once he had the technique sussed, was a skoosh-case for him. As Jimmy swam, he imagined his legs were fused like a merman's tail or the powerful flipper of the albino whale. That way he could make his body ripple through the water without effort. And, of course, he also imagined that the Shadow Shape watched him as he swam. Since he didn't want it to go away, he kept on swimming, perfecting the stroke, motivated to do his best. Sometimes he felt he could swim for ever once he got going, his brain clicking into autopilot.

'Stop there, Jim. You're doing great.'

GI Joe had to tap Jimmy on the head to prevent him pushing off for yet another length.

Butterfly.

Jimmy couldn't believe he was going to swim butterfly! It was always his favourite stroke. To watch, that is. Now he was going to *do* butterfly himself. He was halfway there. More than halfway. GI Joe said the kick was the hardest, getting the rhythm right. And Jimmy could do that in his sleep.

Every swimming pool dream Jimmy had lately made him work a nightshift on whatever stroke he'd been learning during the day with GI Joe, the Shadow Shape lingering, as ever, at the deep end of the pool. Jimmy always checked it was there when he surfaced for air.

And it was, although vague and nebulous, and when Jimmy reached the deep end – as he always did in his dreams now – the Shadow Shape was still too filmy to be identified.

Lately, Jimmy's better swimming dreams took him to the sea. There, the water was always green and cold and salty. In these dreams, Jimmy didn't so much swim as let himself be carried out on waves just bumpy enough to make him cry *whoa* as he rode them.

Ellie was always in these dreams, flitting around Jimmy. A mermaid extension of the Ellie he had seen more of than he could ever have imagined these past few weeks of the holidays: walks in the park, rummages in record shops, she even met Jimmy after swimming some nights . . . In dreams, Ellie's hair floated around her head and arms and shoulders, woven through with pearls and tiny shells. As she swam, the scales of her shimmering tail would coil and flick around Jimmy. She would tug him gently by the hand, bearing him out to sea.

No wonder butterfly kick was a doddle in reality: all Jimmy had to do was pretend he was a merman chasing his mermaid from one end of the pool to the other.

After swimming his first proper fifty metres of butterfly, Jimmy surfaced. GI Joe was chatting to an older bloke who Jimmy had seen coaching Victor on squad nights. Recently, Jimmy had been aware of this man watching him as he swam.

'Are you sure this is Jim *Kelly*?' said the coach bloke. He seemed perplexed by Jimmy's surname, shaking his head doubtfully as he stared down from the edge of the pool, hands folded across his chest. When he tapped his foot, his massive quadriceps muscle leapt up and down under his skin like a piston.

'Definitely *Kelly*?' he confirmed with GI Joe, who shrugged, looking a bit non-committal himself.

Course my name's Kelly, thought Jimmy, heaving himself out of the water in response to a jerk of the head from GI Joe. (No need to clamber up and down the pool steps these days.) This was a daft conversation. What else could it be?

'What age are you, Jim?'

When Jimmy pulled up his goggles he could read the

name, *Barry Dyer, SASA SQUAD COACH* monogrammed on the man's white t-shirt.

'Fourteen,' replied Jimmy

'You're fairly coming on,' said Barry Dyer, matter-of-factly. A short guy, he had to crane his neck back to make eye contact with Jimmy. 'How long's that?'

He addressed GI Joe.

'Four weeks.'

'Five,' Jimmy corrected him.

Barry Dyer looked Jimmy up and down critically, taking in the goggles dangling from his hand and the sleek long-line swimming shorts that GI Joe had bought Jimmy the day he learned backstroke. 'Swimming every day.'

A statement, not a question.

'Watching what you're eating.'

That was another statement, but Jimmy processed it as a question, dropping his head to his chest. A guilty reflex.

'Aye. I can see you toning up, son,' said Barry Dyer, smacking Jimmy on the upper arm. 'And some of the weight's coming off too, but good swimmers can carry a bit extra. No big deal. Mind, you'd come on faster if you trained with my squad. Be glad to have you. I'm one lad short to demonstrate butterfly in this Swimathon coming up.'

Jimmy was still looking down long after Barry Dyer had strode out of sight. What would Victor say to that one? Fat boy invited to join the swimming team? Jimmy wasn't sure if his legs were trembling with pride or apprehension.

GI Joe tried to catch Jimmy's attention with one of his shoulder punches. 'What about that, Jim? Asked me what team you swam for. Says you've a beautiful style. A natural.'

Jimmy still couldn't look up.

Now he was completely gobsmacked. Not only at Barry Dyer's compliments, but at what he could see when he looked down the length of himself.

His own toes.

CHAPTER 22

FAT BOY SWIMMING

It was a Friday night, but not the usual Friday night. It was the night before the Swimathon. Six biscuit tins of tablet and caramel shortcake were stacked in the hall. Two giant saucepans of bolognese sauce cooling by the open kitchen window. One smaller dish sat on the cooker, ready for Aunt Pol when she arrived. In the fridge, dwarfed by the trifles and tiramisus that Jimmy had prepared earlier, was an individual portion of tiramisu soaked in extra Amaretto liqueur and sprinkled liberally with dark chocolate curls.

Aunt Pol's favourite.

But she was very late, arriving, not from work this week, but from Spain where she'd grabbed a last minute break with one of her pals. When Jimmy checked teletext, it showed her plane wouldn't be landing for another hour. Ages yet before she dropped off her suitcases and came round.

Jimmy was restless, pacing the flat. He switched on a CD – Talking Heads – but it made him too jittery. He didn't want that, knowing that if he thought too much about tomorrow he'd get so nervous that he could blow everything.

He contemplated phoning Ellie, but resisted. He'd been on to her for an hour already tonight, and Mum was giving him heavy grief about the phone bill these days.

There was always Friday night TV. All those comedies. Jimmy hadn't watched them lately.

He flopped on the settee but couldn't relax. Nobody was being funny enough to make him concentrate, let alone laugh. Not even Father Ted.

It was no good.

Despite Barry Dyer's advice, *Take it easy. Get an early night,* Jimmy couldn't help himself.

He was much too hungry.

Though not for food.

Leaving a message on Aunt Pol's machine to say where he was, Jimmy plucked his trunks from the pulley and headed for the pool.

'There's a new inflatable in the water.'

Unbelievable, thought Jimmy, pausing as he closed his locker. Would he ever escape these eejits? As Dog Breath expelled a blast of foetid air in Jimmy's ear, Maddo, who Jimmy hadn't seen for weeks now, larked at Jimmy's elbow. He kept knocking Jimmy's hand away as he tried to turn his locker key, but it was a stupid childish gesture rather than a menacing one.

He looks wasted, thought Jimmy, as Maddo pranced in front of him, trying to block Jimmy's route from the locker area to the pool. 'Wanna get past, fatso? Say, "puleeeeeze, Matthew".'

Jimmy ignored them. *Two lengths of butterfly, fast as I can. Good tumble-turn at the end of the first length and the biggest push-off I've ever done,* he'd been chanting to himself as he changed, remembering Barry Dyer's words after the final coaching session: 'Squad's got a real chance with you swimming butterfly for us, Jim.'

Big responsibility.

'These your new drown-faster trunks?'

The tone was snide. But Victor was frowning, not gloating. His mouth was going through the motions while his eyes were all over Jimmy like a rash. He flexed his injured hand, unbandaged now, but scarred purple across the knuckle where the stitches had dissolved. Jimmy reckoned, since Victor hadn't turned up at any of Barry Dyer's dawn training sessions, that this was his first swim for a while. He was clearly seeing big changes in Jimmy.

'What you doing here anyway?' Victor's eyes narrowed, two slits of suspicion. 'Looking for tips from the experts?'

'Telt you Vic,' Maddo tried his joke for the third time, 'he's an inflatable escaped.'

'Shurrit you,' Victor withered Maddo. Like a kicked mongrel, he slunk out of sight.

'What *are* you doin' here, Kelly?'

Jimmy's arms breaststroked a pathway between Victor and Dog Breath. He pointed to a poster advertising the Swimathon.

'Getting in some last minute practice,' he said.

'You're no' swimming races in Barry's squad?' Victor spat after Jimmy in disbelief. But Jimmy didn't turn back to correct him.

The pool was busy, full of families, babies, kids. As usual, everyone second-glanced Jimmy when he appeared. Tall, broad, bulky, still overweight. However, no one giggled, or nudged their neighbour: *Clock that.* There was something too imposing about the way Jimmy chose a float and a leg brick from the crate at the side of the water and went to the cordoned-off section of the pool marked:

Lane Swimmers Only

He set his water bottle on the edge of the pool then dropped like a stone. The instant his feet touched the bottom he plunged underwater and began to swim. Long, strong, steady front crawl. Folk still stared. A few of them nudged each other. But not one person laughed.

Whoa! He fair goes, yon big fellow!

Lovely swimmer to watch.

Like sonar, Jimmy sensed the effect he had on people when they saw how well he swam. That was why he liked to get going quickly in the pool. It felt good to feel good about himself.

It even felt good, with Victor watching. In fact, for some reason it felt especially good. Maybe it was because Jimmy's sonar told him that Victor couldn't believe his eyes at this moment, and had to slip into the pool next to Jimmy and keep pace beside him just to check that fat boy swimming wasn't an optical illusion. Jimmy grinned to himself as he completed the warm-up routine that Barry Dyer had taught him. When he slowed just short of the shallow end, Victor lunged for the wall making a big show of touching it first.

Panting triumphantly, Victor gave Jimmy the finger before kicking off again. Pelting hell for leather up the pool.

I'm not going after him, Jimmy decided. He watched Victor cut his streamlined path to the deep end. I'm saving my energy for tomorrow.

Two lengths of butterfly against the clock, thought Jimmy, and that would do him tonight. He filled his lungs and plunged. He was more than a third of the way up the pool before he surfaced for air. Barry would be well pleased if he did the same at the Swimathon. Now Jimmy brought in his arms, heaving them with all his strength over his head, then ploughing them back into the water. His ears were pulsing to the beat of his own blood. It coursed through him, a rhythm only broken when he surfaced for air, and sampled the high-pitched ricochet of swimming pool squeals against the relentlessness of some forgettable number one pop song.

At the end of the first length, Jimmy tumble-turned. All his coiled weight giving him the momentum he needed to kick off the back wall and fire piston-long through the water for outstretched ages before he needed to take another stroke. Jimmy grinned to himself. He'd felt completely comfortable, swimming those two lengths. What's more, he knew that he still held back that extra something he'd need for tomorrow's race.

Boot.

From nowhere Jimmy's water bottle glanced the

bridge of his nose, shattering his new goggles.

'Smiley show off.'

Maddo, who was rocking back and forth over the edge of the pool, spat his verbal insult at Jimmy. Dog Breath copied him with the real McCoy. It missed Jimmy and landed on Victor's shoulder where it sat like a small green frog.

'Ye clatty bam-pot,' bawled Victor so loud and furiously as he flicked the frog-grog at Jimmy that all the attendants belted towards the shallow end blowing their whistles. Quickly, Victor ducked under the water, tugging Jimmy's trunks down before losing himself in the soup of swimmers.

'Bullseye, Vic!' gurgled Dog Breath.

'Splatto, fatto,' honked Maddo, sinking to his knees as hilarity turned his legs, as well as his brain, to jelly.

Jimmy, eye to eye with Maddo, didn't feel like laughing. He could taste his own blood running from his nose into his mouth.

Oh, no, Jimmy didn't feel like laughing.

'I'm sick of you wasters noising me up.'

Jimmy heaved himself out the pool just as the beefiest pool attendant reached the scene. But Jimmy didn't need handers.

'Don't bother hassling me any more. Right?' Jimmy's order burbled red through his lips, flecking Maddo and Dog Breath. He shook them, not hard, but firmly. A pair of scrapping mongrels that needed a lesson.

Inside Jimmy's chest a furnace roared:

'It's over,' he said. 'Tell Victor it's over.'

Harry, the beefy attendant didn't let Jimmy leave the Leisure Centre until a first aider looked at his eye.

'He's racing butterfly for the Swimathon,' Harry told her. 'Hope it's not going to need a stitch.'

'My old man'll crack up if you don't swim tomorrow,' Harry pumped Jimmy's hand so firmly his eye throbbed. 'I'm Barry Dyer's son, by the way. My old boy never stops talking about what a natural you are. Says you swim like your dad.'

Mixing me up with someone else, thought Jimmy, recalling Barry's puzzlement when they were first introduced. 'My dad never swam.'

Harry found Jimmy a decent set of goggles from lost property, then offered to drive Jimmy home. 'Reassure your mum those two neds are barred.' He didn't mention Victor who, Jimmy realised, must have slipped away unseen. Unpunished. Slimeball!

'I'm fine thanks, Harry,' said Jimmy, and left the medical room to get changed.

The pool was empty now as Jimmy walked around it. Unlit, the water looked inkier than the night sky, fathoms deep beneath a veneer silvered by tiny spotlights in the rafters. Jimmy paused, slightly dizzy as he stared into the still water. Suddenly, its mirrored surface rippled as though someone on the other side had blown across it to catch his attention, rendering the surface molten, like silk. Jimmy blinked. Glanced up, the quick movement making his injured eye stoun. Fingers probing the wound, Jimmy recalled the similar effect of Harry Dyer's handshake. Or maybe his pain was the result of Harry's weird remark nipping his head: *You swim like your dad.*

Jimmy scanned the darkness. Caught a movement at the deep end. He'd swear to it. The Shadow Shape reaching a hand out to him across the yawning water before it disappeared.

CHAPTER 23
SECRETS

Aunt Pol was waiting when Jimmy came home.

'Who the heck gave you that keeker? Not that poultice Swift?'

'Caught my eye on a cupboard in the kitchen.' Jimmy squeezed the lie into Aunt Pol with his hug. Added quickly, 'You look brown. Meet any nice Spanish men?'

Aunt Pol gave a sad little laugh. 'You look different,' she said, eyes narrow. 'And you're away out swimming on a Friday night. You *are* different.'

'I'm racing in the Swimathon tomorrow as well as doing the cooking.'

Aunt Pol didn't comment. Twisted her spaghetti round and round her fork until it all unravelled and fell off. She'd hardly touched it. Shook her head at the tiramisu. Must have Spanish tum, thought Jimmy.

He tried to cheer her up.

'I've lost a stone and a half,' he said, 'and I'm swimming every day. Didn't ever think I'd do that,' he went on, 'but d'you know the weird thing . . .?'

Jimmy paused. Wanted to make sure Aunt Pol was actually listening before he ran the Shadow Shape business by her. After all, he'd never told anyone this. Not even Ellie.

'I've always felt I *had* to swim. I've dreamed about it. For years. Cos there's someone I'm going to meet, or something I'm going to find when I swi . . .'

'What's this, Jim?'

Aunt Pol definitely wasn't right. All her Spanish colour draining away. Lucky Mum's key rattled the lock.

'Cooeee? Anybody home?'

'Visitor in the hall for you, Jimmy,' called Mum much too brightly. She burst into the kitchen, smiling, but through gritted teeth. 'Here's me the daftie thinking you've been down St Jude's helping Father Joseph raise money for those poor wee children in Africa –' Now she bared her teeth. 'But you lied: you've been away swimming to yourself instead.'

Jimmy could tell by the phoney fixed smile on Mum's face that she was raging with GI Joe right now. But she would never show it. You couldn't argue with a priest. It would be like arguing with God.

She was beeling with Jimmy too, the simmering anger in her eyes transmitting a telepathic warning: *How dare you go swimming and not tell me. I'll see you later, boy. Swimming? I'll swim you*!

The brunt of Mum's fury, however, was hurled at Aunt Pol.

'I suppose you knew all about this?'

'Only that he was taking a few lessons again. Thought he'd drop out the same as all the other times . . .' Aunt Pol's voice tailed to a whisper. She winced from Mum's anger as if she'd been slapped.

'Aunt Pol doesn't know anything about my training, Mum,' Jimmy interrupted. He was shocked at the state of Aunt Pol when Mum turned on her. Never seen her look so crumpled, so pale.

'I wanted to swim myself. Nobody made me, and

anyway,' he shrugged, 'what's the big deal?'

He studied the faces around him. Mum: drawn tight with anger. Aunt Pol: chewing colour to her pale lip. GI Joe: hovering in the background, decidedly uncomfortable.

'What the heck, you lot? All I've done is learn to swim.'

Jimmy grinned. Straightened to his full height. Slapped his pecs. Even contemplated giving them a twirl. You should be chuffed, he was thinking. Look at me. I'm different. I'm happy. I'm changing.

But something was going on here. Lurking in the lack of eye contact between Mum and Aunt Pol. Loitering in the sheepish shuffle of GI Joe who looked as though he'd rather be listening to one of Father Patrick's everlasting sermons than standing here.

This isn't about swimming, realised Jimmy. It's about secrets.

'So you're a swimmer after all, Jim,' said Aunt Pol. Her voice was faraway.

'What goes around comes around, eh?' snapped Mum, bitter. '*And* he's got some daft girl on the go, never off the phone to her. Like father like . . .'

Aunt Pol cut Mum off before she could continue.

'You taught him, Joey?'

GI Joe, stepping out from the safe haven of the kitchen doorway, spread his hands apologetically.

'Jim asked me, Polly. Well, I told him I'd only let him help me if I could do something for him. Never thought he'd say swim, but what could I do when he asked? And I swear, he's gifted. Just like . . . I'm sorry, Polly.'

Mum's eyes were out on stalks.

'You know each other?' she and Jimmy asked together.

Joey? thought Jimmy. Aunt Pol had called the dog-collar dude *Joey.* And what the heck was Joey sorry about? In fact, what the heck was going on? Three people Jimmy thought he knew pretty well seemed to have some alternative existence in a parallel universe all of a sudden. They were talking in riddles, and it was doing his head in!

Jimmy looked from one solemn face to the other. The answers were all here, coiled in the silences between Mum and Aunt Pol, curled in the secrets that GI Joe seemed to know.

'What's the big deal doing the Swimathon, Mum?' Jimmy's tone was as light as one of his meringues. 'I'm well fit for it and I've only to do two serious lengths. The rest is just training.'

'Don't want you swimming.' Mum shook the notion from her head, adding lamely, 'With your chest and your skin, and your ears.'

'Can hardly swim without them,' said Jimmy, trying to inject the situation with a bit of levity. 'Anyway, look at me.'

He thumped his pecs again. 'Haven't used my inhaler for weeks. I'm losing weight. You can see *muscles*. I'm feeling brilliant. Why can't I swim? This is nothing to do with my health, is it?'

Jimmy looked to Aunt Pol for support. The hand covering her mouth was shaking.

'Aunt Pol, why shouldn't I swim?'

GI Joe was no help either. He was frowning hard at Aunt Pol, knuckles clamped to his teeth as though he was scared he'd blurt out something he shouldn't.

'I'll let Barry Dyer know Jimmy can't make it if you think that's best,' he shrugged.

There was a beat of silence before Aunt Pol spoke.

'No,' she said. Her voice was strong.

'No,' she repeated. She was looking at Mum. 'Jim's going to swim. But I'm telling him the truth first.'

They put Jimmy out of the kitchen, to have a powwow before they would reveal why they were all acting like characters from some dire daytime soap. He flicked aimlessly through the TV channels.

His stomach gurgled loudly. Nerves. He squashed his fist into his belly. It didn't sink in so far any more; he could detect the contours of his ribcage.

'I'm heading, Jim. Let you folks talk.'

Concern burned in GI Joe's eyes. He looked small tonight, thought Jimmy, who felt he towered over Coach when he rose to walk him out. Maybe it was seeing him in the dog-collar. He even sounded like a priest, voice quiet; compassionate.

'Look,' GI Joe said, laying his hand on Jimmy's forearm. Gentle. No punches.

'If you need to talk – later. Anytime. If there's things

you . . . and you don't fancy swimming tomorrow, just . . . well, I'm here, Jim.'

'Why wouldn't I feel like swimming tomorrow?' Jimmy called after him cheerfully as GI Joe ran downstairs. 'And, hey. How come you know Aunt Pol?'

'School.' GI Joe shouted back. 'Should have been my girlfriend.'

So you'd a thing with GI Joey?

The words were on the tip of Jimmy's tongue but when he saw the state of Aunt Pol he was glad he kept shtoom.

She was even more peely-wally than before; apart from her eyes. They were ringed red from crying.

'What's up?'

Suddenly panicky, Jimmy looked from Aunt Pol to Mum. From her sniffs, Jimmy knew that even Mum – who hadn't shed a tear at Dad's funeral – had also been bubbling.

'Mum? Wait.'

But Mum didn't wait. She pushed past Jimmy gesturing with a flap of her hand that he should stay with Aunt Pol.

'Look at this, Jim,' said Aunt Pol in a tiny voice. She was holding out a small green notebook.

CHAPTER 24
FRANKIE

It was a night when Jimmy teetered on the tighrope of sleep without ever slipping properly into unconsciousness. His mind kept him awake, turning cartwheels, spinning from the chandeliers, tapping out a noisy Riverdance on his skull.

No wonder.

The inside of his brain was like one of those plastic snowstorm ornaments that you shake, sending particles spiralling through a liquid medium. In Jimmy's case, each particle was a fragment of truth, slipping through his reason as he tried to make sense of it.

Mum's not my mum.

Aunt Pol's not my aunt.

Dad wasn't my dad.

My dad was a swimmer.

Like I am.

That was the nub of what Aunt Pol had revealed, tumble-turning Jimmy's world upside down in a few bald sentences. Jimmy barely had his head round any of it when the final particles of the crazy snowstorm settled.

'I'm your mum, Jim, and he's your dad.'

The green notebook lay beside Jimmy on the duvet as he tried to sleep. Photographs. Not many. Newspaper cuttings mostly. They were grainy, ink smudged, paper curled at the edges, yellowing. Old glue discoloured the newsprint, making the articles difficult to read. But the headlines had been clear enough:

Fallon to the Final

Big Frankie Fallon:
New Swimming Hope

CHAMP QUITS

'Frankie Fallon. That's his name, is it?'

Jimmy had been surprised at his outward calm as he flicked back and forth over his ancestry. Inside he was too churned up to read anything properly.

'These are all from before I met him,' Aunt Pol explained as Jimmy turned the pages. 'Your dad swam for Ireland in his teens.'

The same muddy photograph was used on the 'Fallon to the Final' and 'New Swimming Hope' pieces. It showed a line-up of swimmers poised for a dive. One person was unmistakable.

'He could be my twin.'

Hours later, in half-sleep, Jimmy heard himself repeat what he had exclaimed when he first saw his father. That black and white newspaper picture had only hinted at the resemblance between him and Frankie, however. The single colour photograph of him towering over Aunt Pol, arms round her, was unbelievable.

First, the hair. Frankie's if anything, looked even redder than Jimmy's. And longer. Frankie was freckly, even at twenty he was still freckly. Brown eyed, broad-shouldered, beefy, very tall.

And good fun, Jimmy thought, with a pang. There was a twinkle in his dad's eyes.

'He was six two, Jim,' Aunt Pol said. She ran her finger the length of the photograph. 'Foot taller than I am.'

You're not my Aunt Pol any more. What do I call you?

Four in the morning, and Jimmy wondered if, like him, Aunt Pol, who was sleeping over on the saggy settee, was staring into the dawn.

'What am I supposed to call you now?' Jimmy whispered, wishing he could phone Ellie for advice. 'I can't call you mum. Mum's my mum.'

Jimmy was tempted to slip into Mum's room right now. Wanted to hear himself say to her, 'Y'all right Mum?' Because she'd been the most upset of the three of them about this whole business.

She'd given Jimmy a big hug – not like her – and then she'd cried. Told Jimmy she was sorry. Could hardly get the words out, she was so upset. Horrible, thought Jimmy, the replay forcing tears through his own lashes.

'You know me and your dad were only doing what we thought was best, Pauline,' she'd said to Aunt Pol. Or rather, Pauline. Her only daughter, not her wee sister. No wonder Mum's heart was breaking under the weight of a secret like that, wept Jimmy. No wonder she'd shut herself in her room.

Jimmy heard her sniffing for ages before the house grew quiet, but when he knocked her door her voice was back to normal.

'I'm fine, son. Go to sleep now.'

It was daylight when Jimmy slept. And dreamed.

He strode along his street wearing his swimming togs, a crowd following him, all the way to the Leisure Centre. First came Mrs Hughes. She led the English class in a crocodile, reading aloud from Jimmy's essay. En route, Mum's wee wifey pals from St Jude's choir joined in, drowning Mrs Hughes out with their Grand Ol' Oprey rendition of Bowie's 'Heroes'.

Two football teams doing Mexican waves came next, accompanied by Busty and The Tyre dressed as cheerleaders. They paraded up and down the line bearing trays of chocolate éclairs on their heads. Amidst the footballers, wreathed in clouds of cigarette smoke skulked Senga, Chantal, Maddo and Dog Breath.

The crowd swelled as it approached the Leisure Centre. Hamblin was there somewhere and all the obesity consultants Jimmy had consulted over the years in their white hospital coats. Around them danced GI Joe's family from the middle of nowhere.

Jimmy went alone to the pool while everyone else crammed the spectators' gallery. In the first row, dressed like royalty, sat Mum. Dad was beside her, his newspaper covering his face. Aunt Pol was next, looking anxious. And enormously pregnant. GI Joe, at her side, looked much smaller than in real life, his head disappearing into a massive dog-collar so that only his eyes and his stubbly crewcut were visible. He gave Jimmy a cheery thumbs up.

And a whistle blew.

Jimmy turned to the water as a murmur of anticipation filtered through the spectators. There were only two competitors lined up for the heat, himself and Victor Swift.

Jimmy positioned himself to dive, copying the stance of a swimmer he'd seen in a grainy photograph recently. Arms low, weighting the body towards the water. Knees bent. Primed. Ready to spring.

At the deep end, a movement distracted Jimmy. He raised his head.

The Shadow Shape was there. A filmy screen of ectoplasm stretched over Jimmy's horizon, held at one end by Mum, the other end by Aunt Pol. It moved and writhed, semi-transparent, struggling to remain taut and whole as something bigger and far more concrete tore through it. Big Frankie Fallon. Dad.

'Fair play to you, son!' called the huge, red-haired man, cupping his hands to shout the length of the pool.

'See. Telt you my maw said your auntie wasn't your auntie,' said Victor, diving as the whistle blew, leaving Jimmy standing.

'I'm honestly not hungry,' Jimmy insisted, pushing away the toast that Mum had thumped in front of him three times already. It was morning. Swimathon morning.

'You're not swimming on an empty stomach, is he, Pauline? You tell him. You'll faint in the pool, Jimmy. Sink and drown. Talk sense into him. He's as daft as you.'

Jimmy could still hear Mum muttering to herself over the roar of the bathwater.

'She's getting all dolled up to come and see you, Jim.' Aunt Pol drew up a chair and sat close. 'She's that proud you know.'

Aunt Pol, pale, puffy-eyed, lit a cigarette and inhaled deeply before she spoke again.

'I'm proud too. You're the best –' Her chin was wobbling. Tears in her eyes. She was about to break her own nae greetin' rule that she insisted Jimmy follow even when he had every reason in the world to bawl his eyes out. 'Eat. Mum's right, Jim. You've got to eat.'

'Can't,' said Jimmy, although he made an unconvincing show of chewing and chewing a single mouthful of toast. Tasted like cardboard.

How could he eat?

He was full to the brim.

Everything he'd consumed last night lay rich and

heavy like a thick creamy sauce on his heart, on his mind, on his stomach.

Undigested.

And none of it was food.

The space where the Hungry Hole had yawned was crammed at last. Jimmy was so full, so bloated, that his throat ached when he gulped. But he didn't feel satisfied yet. Everything inside needed to settle into place first. Right now his guts were churning.

His head was churning. Everything was churning.

'Jim?'

GI Joe sounded as if he was back in South Africa, his voice was so small on the phone.

'How're things?'

Different.

'OK.'

'And your mum?'

'Which one?' Jimmy was surprised at how quickly – defensively – he snapped back.

There was a long pause, Jimmy sensing GI Joe's awkwardness crackling down the phone line.

'She's fine.' Jimmy softened. 'In the bath, singing. Listen.'

Jimmy carried the phone to the bathroom door to give GI Joe the full flavour of Mum's swoopy 'Amazing Grace'.

'She's happy if she's singing. But we're in a queue out here,' explained Jimmy. 'Legs crossed.'

Relief blasted through GI Joe's laughter.

'So you're still swimming? Don't want me to phone Barry and cancel?'

'And let my granny down?' Jimmy spoke very quietly into the receiver, trying out the relationship for size. Now GI Joe would know everything was out in the open. Better all the same that he wasn't here to see the flush it brought to Jimmy's face.

'Polly. How's she doing?'

'Ask her yourself, Joey,' said Jimmy throwing the handset at Aunt Pol so she couldn't dive into the bathroom before him when Mum opened the door in a cloud of steam.

'Joey. For you, Polly,' he said, feeling as he made a quick cuppa for Mum, that whatever had gone on between Aunt Pol and GI Joe was just one layer of the onion too much for Jimmy to peel away as yet.

'We're all getting there though,' murmured Jimmy to himself waiting for the kettle to boil. For a moment he closed his eyes. The sound of Mum's singing blended with the sound of Aunt Pol chortling deep into the phone. Jimmy smiled.

CHAPTER 25

TITBITS

'Pauline was eight months gone before we knew anything.'

Mum sounded miles away, but only because her head was buried in her wardrobe as she rummaged among her clothes.

'Sit down, son,' she'd said. 'In case we don't get the chance later.'

Then she plunged among her coat hangers, talking above the clatter. Maybe the only way she could do this, Jimmy realised. Turned away from him, busying herself with other things, pretending they were more important. Defense mechanism.

'I must have been blind, not seeing Pauline getting stout. One night I called the doctor out because her back was hurting and she couldn't settle. She takes one look and whips her into maternity.'

'Aunt Pol didn't know she was pregnant? You're joking.'

Mum withdrew from the wardrobe and sighed, looking, not directly at Jimmy, but at his reflection in her dressing table mirror.

'Happens. Still happens. Daft lassies. Concealed pregnancy they call it. A guilty secret, Dad said. Fair knocked his stuffing out. His wee girl. Clever. Set for the Uni. Law she was going to do. Suddenly we're standing over a hospital bed looking at her with a baby in her arms. Fifteen. Helpless. You go into shock.'

Of course, thought Jimmy. That explained the single photograph GI Joe had studied with such interest. Explained why Dad spent the next twelve years – his *last* twelve years – hiding behind a newspaper blocking the sight of Jimmy out. Mum's anxiety in that photograph, watching Aunt Pol holding Jimmy in her arms as if he was a grenade that was about to explode. That made sense too. *And* the blank terror in Aunt Pol's eyes: *What have I done?* No wonder everyone – apart from himself – looked freaked.

'Never met the – him – your father.' Mum made the words 'your father' sound distasteful, twisting her mouth into a grimace as she applied pink lipstick carefully. She kept her mouth half open, moving her lips slightly as if she was rehearsing her next statement. Through the mirror Jimmy watched her intently.

Their eyes locked. Mum's hard, seeing back into memory. Then, under Jimmy's scrutiny, they softened.

Snap.

She closed her mouth. Blotted her lips with a tissue, stifling other things she could say. But didn't.

She sighed.

'Your dad was back to Ireland before you came along. Pauline couldn't get in touch with him. So she said. Dad was all for having the police because Pauline was a minor – fifteen – but Pauline swore your dad thought she was eighteen. Father Patrick was involved, of course. He said we'd have to have you adopted unless we pretended you were mine. Och, it was all mess.'

Mum's shoulders slumped beneath the weight of the secret she had kept all these years. Under her fresh powder and lipstick, Jimmy noticed her age for the first time: the soft wrinkles pouching her face, the droop of her jowl. He'd never thought her old before. She'd always just been Mum. The best.

A wave of affection swept Jimmy, and his arms went round his mum. He squeezed her tight.

'You're glamorous for an old granny,' he said.

Together they sat, shoulder to shoulder, not speaking as they examined each other in the mirror.

'You know, you're right. I'm not bad for my age.' Mum stood up first, dusted herself down. She sounded like Aunt Pol, thought Jimmy. When she grinned and stroked Jimmy's cheek, she even looked like Aunt Pol. Jimmy had never spotted the resemblance before.

DESSERTS

CHAPTER 26
MERMAN

GI Joe was pacing up and down outside the Leisure Centre when Jimmy arrived with Aunt Pol and Mum.

'Just enjoy yourself today, Jim,' he advised, as they parted at the changing rooms. 'You've proved yourself already learning to swim. Never mind winning.'

Aye, that'll be right, thought Jimmy, as he lined up with the other competitors at the poolside. *Never mind winning*! All very noble. Now that he was here, having put in all those hours of training, did he ever want to win this race?

After all, he would *never* have dreamed he'd be in this situation: A competitor.

Next to Victor. With a girlfriend good enough to eat

rooting for him alongside Coach in the spectator's gallery, her dancing eyes never leaving him.

Not to mention the eyes of the five blokes from other swimming clubs, all go-faster goggles and six packs with attitude. They looked along the starting line, clocking the new lardy lad. Sizing him up.

Taking in the height: What was he? Six one? Two?

The new aerodynamic into-the-wood haircut: Crikey! Well mean.

The belly: Massive. Solid, mind.

The breadth: Shoulders like a medieval battering ram.

The reach: Long, powerful-looking arms positioned for the dive.

Five blokes and Victor.

All looking.

Looking worried.

Splash!

A whistle blast and they were off. Jimmy, a torpedo, breaking the surface of the water well ahead of all the other competitors.

Never mind winning, GI Joe tells me after all the training I've put in. Never won squat. Not one certificate for effort in class . . .

Ripple ripple ripple.

Fused together, Jimmy's legs became a merman's tail powering him through the water.

Crash!

Jimmy's arms were plunging pistons driven by the might of his shoulders. As he reared up, gulping air like some huge sea-creature before his next stroke, he heard cheers, and whistles, and yells echoing around his head.

For him. What a sound!

Jimmy was halfway through the race already, approaching the wall at the deep end. He wouldn't surface again until he was a third of the way down the home strait. There was no need to be above the water any more to sense the effect his performance was having on the spectators' gallery. He could feel the atmosphere, the charge of it, crackling the water like static. Yells echoed around him, but there was no time to stop. Freeze the moment. Check if people really were on their feet –

Whoa! Look at that huge bloke go!

No time to see Mum and Aunt Pol clinging to each other, willing Jimmy to win, their hearts beating as hard as his own.

Ellie, fists clenched, chanting, 'Jim, Jim, Jim, Jim . . .'

No time to grin at GI Joe's screech: ***'COME ON THE BIG MAN.'***

Things were very close. As Jimmy flipped for the tumble-turn, Victor was on his merman's tail snapping like a crocodile. For one infinitesimal moment as Jimmy passed him, their eyes met under the water. No other witnesses.

That look of disbelief in Victor's eyes; his realisation that big, fat, useless Smelly Kelly, who five weeks ago couldn't have swum his way out of a trickle of Maddo's piss, was taking the mick here, *that* was better than winning, thought Jimmy, butterflying all the way to the end of the race as though his wings were jet-propelled.

He finished at least a body-length clear of Victor. The six packs still frothed like milkshakes halfway up the pool.

'That's our club record smashed,' Barry Dyer screamed as Jimmy's eyes searched the spectators for Mum and Aunt Pol and Ellie. 'Both of you. First and second. You're not even fit yet, Jim, and that was a PB for you, Victor. Great going, lads!'

Victor ignored Barry, spitting out a jet of water. His mouth moved constantly, although the only words Jimmy could make out over a booming tannoy were, '. . . beaten by that fat loser.'

Ladies and gentlemen, let's hear it for our Scotstown Boys' team. A new club record for 100m butterfly in a sensational demonstration race, won by their new team member . . . Big Jim Kelly!

Spectators were clapping even before the announcement was finished. Aunt Pol had her hands cupped over her mouth and was whooping at the top of her voice. Next to her, GI Joe, punching the air with both hands and yelling in that vein-bulging way of his, looked positively demure. Everyone seemed to be standing up, except Mum, who was dabbing her eyes – and Ellie, who was dabbing her glasses.

So this is what winning tastes like, thought Jimmy, as he scanned the crowd. Must have felt like this for my dad.

It had been a while since Jimmy had felt the swoop of hunger in his belly, but now a tiny pocket of emptiness opened inside him.

Instinctively, he glanced up at the deep end of the pool.

What would he think if he saw me? Would he be proud?

I wish he was here. I wish he'd always been here.

'Hey, cheer up, Jimmy,' said Barry Dyer, 'look round. Remember how this feels – and get used to it.' He seized Jimmy's nearest arm, raised it aloft. A victory pennant.

Unnoticed, beneath a fresh wave of applause, Victor slipped out of the pool.

CHAPTER 27

STICKS AND STONES

'You're gorgeous,' Jimmy crooned under his breath, stealing a final glimpse of Ellie, as she edged her way along the gallery behind Aunt Pol. She wouldn't be outside to meet him when he changed because she had a piano lesson, but before she left him she had leaned over the spectator's barrier to squeeze both his wet hands after the race and tell him he was her superhero. Sweet music! Her glasses had been completely steamed up, Jimmy chortled to himself. 'See you later,' she'd said. Even sweeter music! No wonder he swung through the changing room doors like a gladiator.

'Wasnae right, swimming us against a whale. I couldnae get round his arse to overtake him. See the tidal wave when he dived in? *Help*! *Help*! *I'm suffocating*.

There's no room in here any more.' Victor's damsel-in-distress voice instantly severed Jimmy from his joy. He slunk into the showers aware of one or two swimmers exchanging wry smiles at his expense. But no one laughed.

'There should be a law against flab like that, man. Doesn't his blubber make you boke?'

Sticks and stones'll break my bones but names'll never hurt me, thought Jimmy, mentally chanting the mantra that Aunt Pol had taught him.

And when I'm dead and in my grave, you'll be sorry for what you called me.

Not quite so easy to follow this advice when Victor's insults were sloughing off Jimmy's fit new skin like an acid, exposing the same old Fat Boy Fat underneath.

'Heard this one? What d'you get if you cross a pig with a set of swimming trunks?'

Victor's hand gestured towards Jimmy. 'A PIG, right? – with a pair of ba'-crushin' lycra swimming togs?'

Only the sound of running water broke the silence.

'Easy. *That's* what you get.' Victor hollered raucously, stabbing his finger through the steam.

Victor's humourless laughter ricocheted around the showers, but nobody else joined in. One swimmer nodded towards Jimmy as he left the showers, saying to his mate, 'Why's the big man taking a slagging from that plonker?'

'I know, creamed the pants off him in the pool,' said the other, 'He shouldnae take snash like that.'

Another six pack, towelling his hair, cocked his head at Victor. 'He might be fat, man, but he shafted you big style.'

Five remaining six packs murmured their assent.

'Beat me?'

Victor's voice rose in incredulity. 'Beat me? You jokin' man. Pah!' He spat at Jimmy's feet. Sneered.

'That was all a set-up out there. I let fat boy win.' He lowered his voice. 'See, both his mammys were up there rootin' for him. Couldnae have razzed the saddo in front of them.'

BAM!

Two of the six packs had to dive into empty showers to avoid being bulldozed as Jimmy slammed through them like an international scrum forward. Grabbing

Victor's neck with one hand, Jimmy switched the shower above his head to cold and turned the spray on Victor. Full.

'Let me win, did you? Fancy swimming our race over again? Right here, right now?'

Jimmy could feel Victor's Adam's apple quiver under the pressure of his fingers. He loosened his grip.

'Ready? I'm take you on in the water any time, Victor.'

He worried Victor's neck when he didn't answer, staring hard into Victor's pale blue eyes. They blinked back, cowed, pupils reflecting another hulking face. Angry. Ugly with aggression. Jimmy's own.

Jimmy pushed the image of his angry self away in disgust, reeling Victor off-balance so he slipped and slid, all jaggy knees and knobbly elbows, down the wall to the floor like a slick of shampoo.

'Hey, break it up, big man. He's no' worth it.'

The biggest of the six packs stepped apprehensively between Jimmy and Victor, forming a barrier with his arms to restrain Jimmy from the shivering specimen struggling to his feet under a cascade of cold water.

'Game over,' said the six pack, and Jimmy recalled

Hamblin, the PE teacher, saying the very same thing. Not five weeks ago as he held one boy back from attacking another.

This time, the roles were reversed.

CHAPTER 28

AWRIGHT?

'Awright?' asked Aunt Pol.

Everyone kept asking Jimmy that today, as if he was an invalid or something.

It was the first thing Barry Dyer said when he grabbed Jimmy outside the changing cubicles and thumped him in the chest in delight.

'Y'awright, Jim?'

I was till you punched a hole in my ribcage, thought Jimmy, a heavy shrug the best response he could muster. The sweetness of his victory had been tainted by the violent way in which he had gone ape at Victor in the showers, leaving the taste of self-disgust in his mouth. That wasn't me back there, he thought.

Barry, however, was too excited about something to notice Jimmy's mood.

'You dark horse, you,' Barry was saying, finger and thumb poised to pinch Jimmy's cheek. Jimmy stepped back in time. 'I knew it! *Knew* you reminded me of Frankie Fallon.' Barry contented himself with flexing his huge index finger under Jimmy's nose. 'Here's me thinking I was hallucinating; you looking like that, and swimming the way you do.'

'Who told you?'

Jimmy couldn't *believe* his ears, Barry's words knocking the stuffing out of him more than any thump to the chest. Hadn't *begun* to get his head round any of this real dad business and here was his flipping swimming coach discussing it as though it was the weather!

'Was it him? Did he tell you?' Jimmy pointed accusingly at GI Joe, chatting at the reception desk with Mum and Aunt Pol. Must've been him, thought Jimmy. 'Blabbermouth.'

'You don't mean Father over there?' Barry Dyer looked even more upset than Mum did when Jimmy or Aunt Pol came out with something irreverent. He covered Jimmy's stabbing finger.

'Father never said a word about you,' he whispered. 'Even when I asked him if he believed in reincarnation. Told him you were the spit of this big Irish junior I remembered. "Fallon was the name," I says. "Swear to God that could be him in that pool." And Father Joe says to me, "I'm a priest; don't do reincarnation. And, anyway, Jim's himself. His own man; a one-off."'

Barry gave Jimmy a brace of matching shoulder punches.

'That young lady told me Frankie Fallon was your dad,' Barry said, blushing slightly as he spoke. He was pointing, not at Aunt Pol, but at Mum.

'Awright, Jim?' Now GI Joe wanted to know. 'Because you've got a face like fizz on you. Things OK?' He was nodding towards the showers.

'Sorted,' said Jimmy. 'Victor doing his usual. But ach –' Jimmy's swiped the air as though he was knocking away a pesky midgie.

'Something else up, Jim?'

Jimmy stalled, shoulders slumping. Blurted before he could stop himself. 'All this business about my dad.' He was watching Mum and Aunt Pol laughing with Barry.

'Getting to you now? You want to know more about him?' asked GI Joe.

Jimmy shrugged.

'Dunno. Dunno what I want to know.'

'You've a lot to get your head round, Jim. It'll take time.'

'Everything's so *different,*' Jimmy mumbled, watching Mum and Aunt Pol throw their heads back to laugh at something Barry said. He'd never seen them behave like this before. So chilled. Aunt Pol with her arm around Mum's shoulder shaking her teasingly. Mum primping her hair slightly for what could only be Barry's benefit.

'Must be a relief for them, Jim,' said GI Joe, mind-reading. 'Getting things out into the open.'

'I knew there was something – something, not right. I had dreams –' Jimmy began, but his thoughts and feelings flew about in his head too rapidly to be pinned down. 'I just wish I could see my dad, find out about him,' he whispered, before slipping past GI Joe, and Barry and Mum and Aunt Pol. He needed to get outside for air.

'Awright, Jim?' whispered the priest, touching Jimmy's arm gently. He had found Jimmy leaning against the Leisure Centre wall, his eyes closed.

'I'll tell you one thing I remember about your dad. You couldn't miss him, Jim. He was built like a brick cludgie.'

'You mean he was fat.'

Jimmy's eyes remained closed. He didn't want anything to distract him from the information GI Joe was feeding him.

'First impression, Jim, was this huge fella. Big red mullet of long hair. Frankie was totally different from the rest of us. That's why,' GI Joe admitted, 'I couldn't understand what Polly saw in him at first.'

'See, Jim, back then I'd have eaten myself if I was chocolate. I was a wee poser stringing Polly because I thought I was gorgeous. But I was rotten to her, always arranging dates then standing her up. Blanking her if she spoke to me. Total wally. All flicked hair and attitude. She must have thought I was scum when I turned up here again after all these years. You'll always get teenagers like me, Jim. Run of the mill, ten a penny. But you wouldn't buy two Frankies for a pound.'

'Frankie was different,' GI Joe said. That, thought Jimmy, was one of the adjectives he used repeatedly. Along with words like 'hefty' and 'big-built.'

'*Fat* you mean, yeah?'

'Did I say fat *once*, Jim?' GI Joe was getting a bit worked up. 'I said first *impressions* were of someone huge, but you get used to someone's size, see beyond it when you suss the person inside. I mean, d'you think I keep thinking "he's fat" when I'm with you? How tragic would that make me? Frankie was just different. Polly thought so too. Frankie made her feel special, never mucked her about, never made her feel small.'

'How d'you know all this?' Jimmy asked.

'Because Polly told me all about him when I finally came groveling, *begging* her to go out with me. No chance. "Away and admire your blackheads in the mirror," was about the jist of it for me. She said Frankie wanted to marry her. She'd told him she was eighteen, a law student.'

'Course, I slagged her bigtime for lying. Said Frankie must be dumb to believe her. That's when she fell out with me. Never spoke to me again.'

'So you became a priest?'

'I'm daft, Jim, but I'm not stupid.' GI Joe had slapped his big paw so hard on Jimmy's shoulder that his teeth rattled.

'Sure, I took the hump when Polly gave me the cold shoulder. Thought, I'll show her. Chucked in school. Joined the army. Just sixteen. Wee eejit. Didn't come home for five years, not even on leave. Asked to get sent all over the place. *That's* when I found my vocation. Some of the things I saw –'

GI Joe was staring into the horizon. Miles away.

'Nothing to do with Polly. Or Frankie. Although I suppose I owe them.'

'Awright, Jimmy?'

Jimmy had no idea how long Senga and Chantal had been watching him. After GI Joe had gone, Jimmy remained outside trying to picture a teenage Aunt Pol with Frankie Fallon. Was his dad as smitten with his girl as Jimmy was with Ellie, he wondered, smiling a lovestruck smile at the memory of Ellie squeezing his hands. That was when he heard sniggering and opened his eyes. Like a pair of smoking wally dugs, Senga and Chantal were perched on the two walls outside the Leisure Centre, sizing Jimmy up.

'Thenga thinkth you look like Ronaldo wi' your hair cut short like that.'

'Shurrit, did no'. Said ah bet he *thinks* he looks like Ronaldo but he's more like a spacehopper.'

Senga dunted Chantal so hard that she fell off the wall on to her knees.

'Saw you swimmin' through the windae,' said Senga.

'Thenga thaid you made Thwifty look like a pure thaddo. Thenga thinkth you're no' bad lookin' now you're no' tho fat . . .'

Before Chantal could report any more of Senga's musings, Aunt Pol appeared.

'That's his real maw, Swifty says,' Senga informed Chantal in her loudest whisper. 'Swifty says you canny blame her pretendin' she didnae have a son like that.'

Jimmy sensed Aunt Pol bridle, gather breath, about to speak. Instead, she held Jimmy's arm tightly, and they walked away.

'Sticks and stones, remember. That pair are nothing. Ignore them.'

She squeezed Jimmy's arm tightly.

'Awright, Jim?'

There was that dumb, dumb question again.

All Jimmy's anger and confusion simmered over before he could put a lid on it. He threw off Aunt Pol's arm, and yelled into her face. 'No, I'm not actually. How would you like non-stop slagging like that? If it's not my weight, it's my background. I'm supposed ignore it, am I? Can't even take a shower without that prat Victor taking the mick. So I've to play the heavy to keep him off my back, and I hate doing that. Then his dolly-dimple girlfriend starts on me. Nothing's right.' He wasn't finished either.

'Not only am I big fat Jimmy, but to make things worse, everyone in the world except me knows you're my real mum, and Mum's my gran. Oh, and my dad wasn't my real dad. But my real dad ran off and left you up the duff. Still think I'm alright – *Mum*?'

Half-sobbing as he gulped great uneven breaths of air, Jimmy stumbled off.

'Jim, wait. I'm sor –' Aunt Pol called after him. For the first time ever, Jimmy ignored her.

Aunt Pol caught up with Jimmy in the park. She steered him to a bench. The same one where he'd sat with GI Joe. Only weeks back. None of this had happened.

'Here's the only other picture I've got of Frankie. You keep it.'

'But this is me –' began Jimmy, taking the photograph Aunt Pol handed him before he realised that the strip of school tie beneath the treble chin was different from the one Jimmy had worn to St Jude's Primary at that age.

Hair: Longer, redder than his own.

Eyes: Brown like his, maybe a little fairer around the lashes. Kind. Guarded.

Freckles: A myriad.

Nose: A jelly tot squashed between –

Cheeks: Pendulous. A pair of bulging fat sacs straining the skin to a shine.

Chins: Multiple.

Mouth: Fuller than Jimmy's. Generous lips, well shaped. Smiling the non-smile of one for whom being photographed is akin to the infliction of physical torture.

Jimmy turned the photograph over:

Francis Anthony Fallon
St Aidan's Primary, Enniscorthy
June 1975

Words printed carefully in best school handwriting. Scored over the letters, in thick red crayon, a different hand had written:

FATTY

Like father, like son, thought Jimmy.

'Hey, no more secrets, Jim,' whispered Aunt Pol, closing Jimmy's hand around the photograph. 'Promise.'

CHAPTER 29

'MY KITCHEN!'

'Oy! Swifty! Come and get a load of this. Kelly's in there with all that grub.'

'Keekaboo, fat boy!'

'Shhh! Listen! The big tube canny hear you; he's singin'.'

'And dancin'!'

Jimmy's inbuilt radar, normally twitching at the first scintilla of trouble from Victor and co., was blocked tonight. He was way too preoccupied, trying to put the final, final touches to the post-Swimathon feast. Then getting himself the heck away from the Leisure Centre before any guests arrived. This was not GI Joe's plan, of course. He was expecting Jimmy to stick around, planning that Jimmy be unveiled as chef at the end of the night. However, Jimmy, despite Aunt Pol's new no more secrets maxim still had one he wanted to keep to himself. OK, so Busty might have spread the word about his chocolate éclairs in the staffroom, but coming out as a cook was one leap too far. Things were going well enough for now.

He *was* singing. And having a little shimmy to himself, using a coordinated heel-toe dance step to side-slide the length of his kitchen counter. Tucked under one arm like a bongo drum, he held a giant tub of fresh basil. With his free hand, he plucked at the leaves, scattering them from a height on the tomato and mozzarella salads plated before him in time to the music in his head.

Jimmy knew he'd done good. There'd be no complaints tonight. Adjusting the seasoning of the bolognese sauce bubbling on the hob, he ska-stepped across the kitchen to shave extra chocolate curls on six giant bowls of tiramisu.

GI Joe would be well chuffed with the money this feast would raise for the middle of nowhere. And he'd understand that if Jimmy wasn't physically here, there was no chance of anyone spotting him in the kitchens and demanding a refund: *I'm not eating anything that tub of lard's touched.* Folk were squeamish, after all. Easily put off their chuck: a caterpillar on the cress, a hair in the soup, a fat chef cooking. Even those who knew Jimmy could swim out of his box now could be squeamish.

Of course, from a selfish point of view, Jimmy himself didn't want to be around either. He wasn't going to let anyone's distaste taint the memory of today. One of the best days he could remember.

Not only had he won the butterfly, but all afternoon he'd been Jim the Chef. The Maestro. In his element. Magic, it had been.

He'd given orders to GI Joe for a change instead of taking them: 'No, not those plates. Jeezo, Coach! For soup? And surely you can carry more than that!'

He'd dispensed advice instead of receiving it from Mum and Aunt Pol: 'Put a big bowl of Parmesan on every table. And don't serve my bread till the last minute so it's still warm.'

He'd even managed some staff training: 'Ellie, if you

give me your hand, I'll show you exactly how thin to slice the mozzarella. Good. But let's do one more together just to make sure . . .'

Nothing should be allowed to spoil an afternoon like that.

It was lucky that the skewer which Jimmy was using to test the liqueur distribution in his tiramisu was not still in his mouth when Victor shoved his face into the bottom of the nearest bowl. And held Jimmy down.

'You greedy pig. Eating grub that's to feed Coach's wee blackies.'

'Saw you dancin', Kelly,' snorted Dog Breath into Jimmy's ear.

'Just like Baloo,' hissed Victor as Maddo's elbow stabbed at Jimmy's side.

They were wasting brain cells they couldn't afford to lose on these insults. Jimmy wasn't listening. He was too angry. *One dessert ruined,* was all he was thinking. *Thirty portions in it.* He hadn't made any extras.

'Just get out of my kitchen, you lot. I've told you to give me peace,' Jimmy roared, rearing to his full height. He whirled round at speed to face Victor, shaking chocolate and sponge from his face and hair like a lion shedding slivers of prey from its mane. Spattered, Victor, Maddo and Dog Breath retreated one slinking step.

'What d'you mean, *your* kitchen?' sneered Victor.

He watched Jimmy wipe cream from his eyes, flick his fingers clean.

'You not gonny lick yourself?' Maddo ventured, making Dog Breath snicker.

'Shurrit,' snapped Victor, but he sounded uneasy. Jimmy was advancing. '*My* kitchen,' he repeated, forcing Victor to scuttle backwards and off balance through the swing doors into the function room. From the far end, Jimmy spotted GI Joe, charging like a bull elephant towards the scene of the commotion. But Jimmy was going to have this situation sorted well before Coach arrived.

'I'm the chef here tonight.' Jimmy's voice was as firm as his stare.

'No way,' said Dog Breath.

'Liar,' spat Maddo. He shoogled a second bowl of

tiramisu at Jimmy. 'Come on, Fatty. You were just hungry.'

Only Victor said nothing, although his eyes, travelling the length of Jimmy, then glancing behind him to the spread in the kitchen beyond, spoke volumes: *You* really *are the chef.*

CHAPTER 30
CLOSING RANKS

'Best Jimmy goes home too,' said Father Patrick, watching GI Joe clear tiramisu from the floor, and Jimmy rinse it from his face and head under the kitchen tap. 'Let him calm down now those troublemakers are sorted.'

Father Patrick's face wore the *what's that doing here*? expression of someone who's just taken a bite out of something and discovered half a dead mouse.

'In fact, Joseph, I'd say it's unwise for the lad to be – you know – actually *here* during the function at all.' Father Patrick twiddled his wrists like a second-rate magician: *Ali Zoom. Begone, Fatso*.

It was already too late. The function room was filling up. Jimmy would have to stay. Because of the carry-on with Victor, things were running behind.

'Don't worry. I'll make sure nobody sees me,' murmured Jimmy. He turned his back on Father Patrick, stirred his bolognese.

'You will not!'

Ellie's voice rang through the kitchens. Both spec lenses opaque with steam, she looked up from the two boiling cauldrons of spaghetti she was supervising.

'Why would you do that, Jim?' chipped in GI Joe, a 'Sexy Momma' apron jazzing up his priest's suit. 'Tonight's your night to get credit for the way you've used those talents of yours.' He lowered the pile of plates he was carrying and set himself between Father Patrick and Jimmy, arms folded. 'In fact,' he added bearing down on the old priest, 'I've just given our friend Swift a rollicking on that very subject. You're so busy bullying other folks, I told him, unlike Jim Kelly, who's worked his backside off these last few weeks –'

'Literally,' interrupted Ellie.

'– that your *own* special God-given gifts are withering away. Time you took a long hard look at yourself, Victor. Maybe pinched a leaf out of Jim's book.'

Victor's gonna love hearing that, gulped Jimmy to himself. He watched GI Joe fully pumped up into Angry Coach mode, backing Father Patrick towards the kitchen doors. Before the old priest tumbled outside, Mum stuck her head through the hatch. 'Barry's seen those neds off. That Swift lad's shouting his mouth off telling folk he caught Jimmy eating my puddings. "*My* puddings?" I told him. "My Jimmy's puddings, you wee nyaff," I told him. Him and his nippy-faced mother both!'

Aunt Pol's head joined Mum's in the serving hatch. 'That's them barred anyway. Time to serve up. Are you all on strike?'

Father Patrick cleared his throat, and gestured towards Jimmy. 'I was suggesting, Maeve, it might be better if Jimmy stays – keeps out – I mean, if people *see* –'

'See what?' Aunt Pol was through the kitchen's swing doors like a tornado.

But, for once, even she wasn't fast enough at springing to Jimmy's defence. He had a new champion.

'Are you on about Jimmy's size?' Ellie, glasses off,

eyes dancing more pugnaciously than a boxer's feet in the ring, abandoned her spaghetti.

'You like his cooking, but don't like to look at him? No wonder he has to put up with hassle from twits like Victor if folk like you, who should know better, treat him like some kind of outcast.'

As Ellie spoke, Aunt Pol nodded agreement.

'*Very* Christian,' Ellie was saying, 'keeping someone under wraps because he doesn't look like Brad Pitt.'

Jimmy caught Mum's wince, but she didn't say anything.

Father Patrick, opened his mouth to object. 'Young lady –' he began, but Ellie cut through him.

'I mean, you're hardly a skinny-malink yourself, but nobody tells you to stay at home.' Now she whirled around at GI Joe. 'He's bald, and she –' Ellie waved her finger vaguely at Mum and Aunt Pol, but thinking better of it pointed diplomatically to someone beyond the hatch, 'and that woman, she's lame, and he's got a hearing aid, and I've got funny eyes. So what?'

Ellie's funny eyes were blazing, cheeks pulsing.

'There's stacks more to Jimmy than what you see. He's fun. He knows *everything* about music. And he can sing. And he's going to have his own restaurant one day. And he will, because he's an amazing cook.'

'Too right,' Aunt Pol chipped in. She stood alongside Ellie.

'And he's a cracking swimmer,' added GI Joe, finding his voice.

'Got a lot going for him, my Jim,' added Aunt Pol.

'If more people bothered to look beyond what they see.'

Ellie, having said her piece, stuck her glasses back on, and drained her spaghetti.

'We're just trying to protect the lad,' said Father Patrick, appealing to Mum for support.

'Keep him to yourself, more like,' muttered Aunt Pol. 'In tablet and cakes.'

'Don't you start, Pauline,' Father Patrick turned on Aunt Pol, 'You're hardly an example to the boy.'

'Meaning?'

'Hey, not here.' GI Joe raised his arms like a referee. If he'd had a whistle he'd have blown it. 'We're lucky

Jim's still here at all. Everyone talking as if he's invisible.'

Jimmy shrugged, awkward and exposed. It was a disappearing moment. 'I can head,' he said, 'Everything's ready anyway. Just needs served. I'll come back and do the washing up.' 'Think that's best, son.' Father Patrick, nodded approvingly, easing Jimmy towards the kitchen's back door.

'You've got to stay.' Ellie dived for Jimmy, catching his arm.

'Of course he has,' said Aunt Pol. 'We're sick of secrets.'

'He *is* staying,' said Mum, 'or we're all leaving with him.'

'Who's leaving?' bellowed Treesa from the choir, choosing that freeze-frame moment to stick her head through the hatch. 'There's gonny be a rammy out here if we don't get some food. What's keeping you?'

'Waiting for chef's signal,' said Mum. Brushing Father Patrick aside with a glare, she marched Jimmy from the back door to the kitchen hatch so that Treesa could see him.

'Your Jimmy? Chef? He's no'? Girls, away and see this.'

Treesa beckoned the rest of the wee wifeys until the serving hatch was clogged with curious faces.

'There's Maeve's big lad.'

'Jimmy helpin' you, Maeve?'

'He's not helping us. We're helping him. He's our chef!' Mum shouted the wee wifeys down.

'He's no'.'

'In the name of the wee man.'

'Your Jimmy?'

'*Our* Jimmy,' called Aunt Pol. 'Made everything you'll eat tonight.'

'And anything you think I've ever made,' added Mum. She shrugged. 'I've stolen his thunder long enough.' She put her arm around Jimmy's shoulder. Proud as punch.

There was an unprecedented moment of silent contemplation among the ladies of St Jude's choir. They looked from Jimmy to Mum to each other and back again in disbelief.

Treesa, as usual, broke the silence.

'Well, chef, I could eat a scabby dug,' she said, 'Get a jazz oan!'

CHAPTER 31
JIGGING

'No refunds, then, Jim?' said GI Joe, carrying through the last empty plates for washing up.

But plenty of complaints. About the mingy helpings of Jimmy's tiramisu.

'They're licking the patterns off the plates,' said Aunt Pol.

'Balls up,' Jimmy said. He was washing up as Ellie dried. 'I should have grabbed that bowl from Maddo in time.'

'Nah, Jim,' said GI Joe. 'Away you go, I've told anyone moaning about the size of their portions. I say last time I saw folk this wound up over food, my kid's'd missed two deliveries of grain. Get real! You've done a magic job here, Big Man.' GI Joe punched Jimmy on the shoulder, drawing him to the serving hatch. 'Got my message across, showing folk what it's like to want and not get. Ach, and they're a great crowd. Look at them all, giving it laldy on that dance floor.'

'You youngsters get out here and dance!' Mum, waltzing by in Barry Dyer's arms, called through the hatch.

No way, thought Jimmy, even though it looked like fun and practically everyone he could see apart from Mum had two left feet.

'We couldn't keep up,' said Ellie.

Besides, thought Jimmy, It's much better in here.

All the washing up done, he'd turned out the kitchen lights so folk couldn't see through the hatch. He and Ellie stood in the dark, sipping Cokes, heads close because of the noise beyond. Talking.

'Just think,' said Ellie as GI Joe was dragged off to dance by with Aunt Pol, 'if they'd ended up together, there'd be no you.' She nudged Jimmy playfully, her touch arrowing a shiver from his head to his feet as though he'd taken a bite out of an extra-frozen ice lolly.

'Couldn't see them working out,' said Jimmy. 'Coach is too much of an Action Man for her. He's square bashing her round the floor. You can't keep that up in stilettos.'

Jimmy superimposed his Shadow Shape in place of GI Joe. *Mum and Dad,* he mouthed. Had they ever danced together? Had Frankie ever held Pol's hand high and let her spin under his arm?

'Popular guy, is Action Man,' said Ellie. 'Look, people keep slipping him money.'

'He doesn't mess about,' said Jimmy, with admiration. 'Gets things done.'

'Like you,' said Ellie, matter-of-factly.

Jimmy gulped, grateful that the dark kitchen hid his blushes.

Here's your *chance to get something done, you balloon. Put your arm round her. Say 'Are you paying me a compliment?'*

The first chord of a jig obliterated Jimmy's advice to himself. Although his arm ached like a phantom limb to be around Ellie's shoulder, he seemed to have been struck with rigor mortis.

'Get things done? Me? You're joking.'

He sneaked a sideways glimpse at Ellie. She was smiling, biting her thumbnail between her teeth, eyes jumping as she watched Mum organise dancers into sets of six. Jimmy was still staring at Ellie when her smile faded.

'One more,' Mum was beckoning. 'Come on, hen. You're not hiding in there all night.'

Despite Ellie backing herself into the darkness, she was dragged on to the dance floor.

'I can't do this,' Ellie pleaded as the music started and Aunt Pol yanked her sideways in a wide and energetic circle.

Ellie was no twinkletoes, but as the pattern of the dance birled and twirled her, Jimmy held her in his sights. Utterly mesmerised.

Her hair was his marker, so chocolate-mousse fluffy and full, it landed long after the rest of her and all the other dancers had managed a *pas de bas* or whatever step Mum kept yelling at her to do. When the music ended and everyone turned to cheer the band, Jimmy watched Ellie weave across the dance floor.

She's looking for me. She's looking for me, beat the tattoo of his heart in its ribcage as Ellie approached him waving, smiling.

'I'm exhausted!' Ellie sank against Jimmy, her hands spread on his chest just long enough to induce another bout of rigor mortis. It stiffened the arms that ached to cup her shoulders and pull her close.

CHAPTER 32

FIRST LAST DANCE

Nobody actually spotted Victor's graffiti until the end of the night when the lights went up in the function room, and Father Patrick creaked on to the stage to call – in his gloomiest funereal tone – a vote of thanks.

'Blah! Blah! Blah!' Aunt Pol groaned in Jimmy's ear, grabbing his arm as he passed her. 'Go and tell that old goat to put a sock in it, Jim,' she giggled. Then suddenly inhaled cold air through her teeth, tightening her grip on Jimmy's arm.

'He's not that bad –' Jimmy began, nudging Aunt Pol. Then he realised that she wasn't looking anywhere near Father Patrick, or the stage. Nor was anyone else.

They must have hung two dozen of the Swimathon

posters that afternoon, Ellie and GI Joe, while Jimmy set the tables up with fancy napkins and candles. They were all round the function room walls, Barry Dyer lending them the multicoloured pennants from the pool to frill them.

'Really festive-looking!' Mum had proclaimed when she saw what they were doing. 'Your hall's going to look great!'

With the lights down, all the posters probably did say **SWIMATHON**, which is why nobody noticed what Victor's yellow highlighter pen had scrawled over the David Hockney blue of the Leisure Centre pool until the end of the evening. Altering every poster to read:

SWIMATHON

SWIM-A-TON

ROLL-UP, ROLL-UP!
SEE SMELLY KELLY

'Disgusting!'

'Obscene!'

'Who would do this –?'

Instinctively, Jimmy retreated one, two, three steps towards the dark kitchen, aware of Aunt Pol tearing down two posters at once. Barry Dyer charging to the back of the room to do the same. Treesa beside him getting the wee wifeys on their feet. 'C'mon ladies.'

Father Patrick, always slow to catch on, and used to folk fidgeting while he spoke, raised his voice and tapped the microphone. 'One person we mustn't forget,' he intoned, oblivious to the reason why everyone in the room, except the band and Jimmy, was facing the walls, 'is someone whose light has languished under a bushel far too long. Tonight, I want him up on this stage, so we can all congratulate him, not only for his cooking but for his marvellous performance in the swimming pool. So, come on Jimmy Kelly. Don't be shy. *We* see you –'

Jimmy shrivelled inside, eyes on the outstretched signposting palm of Father Patrick.

'Let's hear it for chef,' shrieked GI Joe at Coach pitch, 'Hip, Hip – *Get him out of here,*' he hissed at Ellie, shoving

Jimmy through the swing doors to the kitchen before he knew what was happening.

As the first HOORAY waxed and waned in the dull swish of the door, Jimmy found himself in the fresh air. He seemed to be holding Ellie's hand tight, although he couldn't for the life of him remember grabbing it.

'Nightmare,' gulped Jimmy, 'folk hearing I'm chef then seeing those posters. Turn their stomachs.'

'Och, they all know you're chef now,' Ellie said. 'Your Mum's pal, Treesa, had the word round before anyone tasted a spoonful. Nobody's bothered. They're on your side. Proud of you. Listen, they're cheering you.' Ellie touched her finger to Jimmy's lips until the final Hip Hooray died away, then whispered, 'You deserve it.'

They stood on the kitchen doorstep, flanked by wheelie bins gaping rubbish, leaking spaghetti.

Still holding hands, thought Jimmy. How did that happen?

He stepped into the concrete yard. Enclosed by a high wall, it was practically pitch black, useless light filtering through a barred kitchen window. Clouds scudding the moon obscured any stars that might be twinkling down. The gentlest of drizzle fell.

Summer rain. Jimmy turned his face upwards to catch it. He breathed in its freshness, cool on his warm cheeks.

Ellie's shoulder brushed the skin of his arm, the thrill of her touch forcing every hair follicle on Jimmy's body to stand to attention. Inside the hall a waltz began, carried on the plangent notes of an accordion.

'Last dance.' Ellie squeezed his fingers gently.

Afraid to take the moment further, Jimmy offered no response. *Last dance, cloth-ears,* a voice hissed so loudly through Jimmy's head that he was sure Ellie must hear. *Don't you hear the lady? Your first last dance.*

And she's asking.

All you have to do is turn your feet forty-five degrees to the right and you'll be face to face.

Just the two of you.

Piece of cake . . .

Unless you were Jimmy Kelly:

She'll push me away . . .

Tell me to piss off . . .

My hands are sweaty . . .

I must have BO . . .

Jimmy Kelly would still be in the middle of that dingy yard inventing excuses why he couldn't make a move if Ellie hadn't taken matters into her own hands. She turned Jimmy to face her, took his other hand in hers.

And that was all too much for Jimmy's innate macho pride. It elbowed past all Jimmy's reservations and took over.

Jimmy's arm lifted to Ellie's shoulder. He drew her to him.

It was delicious. The top of her head barely reached his collarbone. Jimmy only had to tilt his face to gorge himself on the smell of her hair, feel all the springy tendrils which haloed her head tickle his cheeks and lips.

'I can't dance,' giggled Ellie as she and Jimmy shuffled around in a circle between the dustbins in the drizzle. Her arms reached two-thirds of the way around Jimmy's waist. He could taste her hair against his lips.

'You'll do,' said Jimmy, his voice strange and deep and faraway. Then his lips found Ellie's in the dark.

Inside the hall, the accordion closed the night with a wistful chord. Cheers from the revellers drifted to the yard where not even a shadow betrayed two figures kissing in the soft rain.

BITTER SWEETS

CHAPTER 33
OCEAN VIEW

Tonight was supposed to be a celebration.

'A *Hurray! Jim and his Smelly Feet are Moving Out My Flat* Party,' Aunt Pol joked in the taxi on their way back to Mum's. Half in fun, she was, and wholly in earnest. First decent laugh they'd shared since Jimmy went to live with her. It had only been three weeks, but it felt like an eternity to Jimmy. This summer, instead of Mum having a few nights in Blackpool with the wee wifeys, she had accepted an invitation from her new beau, the Merry Widower, as Aunt Pol called Barry Dyer, and jaunted off on a tour of Ireland.

A wee trial run for you and Pauline, Mum had called Jimmy's new longer-term living arrangements with Aunt Pol. *See how things work out.*

They hadn't.

Which was why – and although Jimmy had felt pretty guilty admitting this to himself – tonight was to be something of a private celebration for him too. He was coming home. Where he belonged. To Mum. To his kitchen. He'd been stifled at Aunt Pol's. Not just literally, because Aunt Pol lived in a tiny bedsit and Jimmy didn't even have his own bed, and had to wait until Aunt Pol was tired before he could get his head down on her settee, and she sat up half the night. Smoking all over him. Watching old movies . . . But Jimmy had also been stifled by Aunt Pol's efforts to embrace her new role and mother him. Smother him more like! Worse than Mum had ever done. Aunt Pol would barely let Jimmy out of her sight this weather, only allowing him to squad training, or to see Ellie under strict curfew.

'Nine o'clock she wants me back in. Spiff, spiff. It's still the flipping summer holidays,' he had complained to Ellie. More than once. 'I'm fifteen now. We know fine what *she* was up to at my age.'

'Well, you know why she's being so strict with you, Jimmy. Just doesn't want history repeating itself.'

'I'm hardly going to get myself pregnant, am I?'

'Hey, she's only trying to do her best.'

It was funny. Smart Ass Ellie *and* GI Joe kept giving Jimmy the same explanations for Aunt Pol's Gestapo police tactics.

It had been the main topic of Jimmy's last conversation with the priest, the day he went back to the middle of nowhere.

'Don't give Polly a hard time because things aren't the way they were. She's doing her best. Doesn't want to see you make the mistakes she made and it's a right tough call for her to get the balance right. Just you think of the guilt she's carried around for fifteen years. It's in another league from your cooking secret. She's watched you, loved you. From a distance. Thinking, *you're really mine, but I can't tell you that in case you hate me.* Nightmare.'

GI Joe, who had been packing his tatty shorts and t-shirts in a case while he gave Jimmy this sermon, had turned. Laid both paws on Jimmy's shoulders. Digging in. Then he relaxed his grip and gave Jimmy a bear hug. Squeezed him so hard there were tears in both their eyes.

'You better write, Jim,' he warned.

'Soon as something interesting happens,' Jimmy promised.

Jimmy wished GI Joe could be here tonight. Ellie at least. But Aunt Pol had been having none of that when Jimmy suggested it.

'You see too much of her. She's turning your head.'

'But this is a party,' said Jimmy before Mum arrived home with Barry. He'd made celebration scones. Mum would smell them from the bottom of the close and know Jimmy was home.

'Still warm,' he said, folding Mum in a hug, while Barry Dyer crushed his fingers in a friendly handshake. 'Come and eat,' Jimmy squeaked.

'Later, pet,' Mum said. Awful quiet, thought Jimmy. Didn't even get her coat off. Something to show him, she said. 'You too, Pauline.' Mum sat Jimmy between herself and Barry on the saggy settee.

'Look, son,' Mum said, eyes watching Jimmy's face. Her hand was trembling. Barry had to help her support the brochure she was holding open: *Ireland. Hotels and Guest Houses* the cover read.

'We found your dad,' Mum whispered.

Jimmy had no idea how long he stared at the brochure, scared to take his eyes from the page, scared to blink in case the photograph of Frankie Fallon's face disappeared, devoured by Jimmy's hungry eyes.

Frankie Fallon

Proprietor

Ocean View Hotel, Dingle Bay

Everyone in the room was watching Jimmy as he read the caption beneath the photograph, no one more intently than Aunt Pol. Curled up in Dad's big winged chair, nail-gnawing, her eyes searched Jimmy's face. Seeing him find the face he'd been looking for.

His own face, really. Older, bearded. It stared back at him. Still freckly. Half-smiling. Jimmy committed every detail of his father's grown-up image to memory, hanging it in a space in his head where he'd always see it.

'Lives in Dingle Bay,' said Mum. 'Looks out at the Atlantic. Beautiful.'

'"In the name of the wee man, there's Big Frankie Fallon," I said to Maeve.' Barry was bursting with the need to interrupt. 'We were staying in *his* hotel. Would you credit it? "I saw you swim," I says to him when I paid the bill. "You were a champ." "Sure now, that was going back a bit," Frankie says to me. He blushed.'

'Double of you, son. Same lovely smile. Fine big man.' Mum's voice had been quiet at Jimmy's side, hand taking his. Squeezing.

'We didn't say a word about . . . to him . . . just thought we'd let you know.'

'For what it's worth, *I'd* want to know if I'd a lad like you somewhere, Jimmy,' Barry Dyer had added, gruffly. Flustered by the spontaneity of his compliment, he swallowed a scone whole.

If only the Swimathon had raised enough dosh to buy computers as well as a new roof for the middle of nowhere, Jimmy could have e-mailed Coach tonight: *They've found my dad. What do I do now?*

*

So what now, Coach?

Some homecoming celebration. Here was Jimmy, first night back in his own room, in a proper bed, and he couldn't sleep a wink. His Shadow Shape had substance, had life now. He wasn't just some face in an old photograph, or another person's recollection. He was within Jimmy's reach. Yet in some respects, he'd never been so untouchable.

I mean, what if he has a wife, other kids?

Dawn was breaking when Jimmy wrote that first letter to GI Joe.

He might not want to know me.
What should I do?

CHAPTER 34

LETTER FROM THE MIDDLE OF NOWHERE

Jim,

Take your time before you do anything about your dad. Get your head round finding him first. Talk to your Mum, Polly, Ellie. Say what you feel about things. If you do decide to get in touch with Frankie, it's best to go through someone else first. I'll be your intermediary if you like. But there's no rush.

It was magic to get a letter so soon. Never thought I'd get homesick for Glasgow, but it's been some summer! We got things done, didn't we, Jim?

And you're still up at the crack putting in those lengths before breakfast? Brilliant.

Make sure you say hi to Barry. He's doing salsa

classes with your Mum now, is he? Good on them both.

I'm sending photos of my new roof. You'll get them on the school noticeboard for me? It's looking good, yeah? Watertight – well, no rain yet. Say a prayer.

You're up on my wall, by the way, between Mother Theresa and Nelson Mandela. Above Bono. My kids want to know all about you: Are you famous?

No, I tell them, although he might be one day. He's my friend Jim, from Glasgow. Uses his talents to make things happen.

Helped put this new roof over our heads. Then I tell them the whole story . . . cracks them up!

I've sent a loads of info to Mrs Hughes so she can get working on that Link project with Ellie. Tell them both it's a great idea.

And listen, will you tell Victor I was asking for him? Say Coach says 'Use it or lose it'. He knows what I mean.

Keep in touch.

Love to Polly.

Cheers,

Coach

PS. Thanks, Jim. For everything.

CHAPTER 35

NOT THE LAST CHAPTER

'What was that out there? Opposition think it's Christmas! And you. Aye you, Kelly, you big balloon. Ye'd need a white stick to miss a save like that.'

Bursts of rowdy laughter from the guest changing room next door intensified the pall of silence that fell at Hamblin's entrance.

Just like old times.

Hamblin's sardonic blue gaze swept the room, homing in on his favourite target. Jimmy, exposed in his underwear, blushed scarlet from his toenails to the roots of his hair.

'All you had to do was block the goal, Kelly,' Hamblin said ponderously, inflating himself to fill the changing room doorway.

'Jeezo, I put you there because you're wide. Just had to s-p-r-e-a-d yourself out. Shuffle to the left. Shuffle to the right. Never asked you to run. Is standing still too much for you?'

Hamblin, licking spittle from his lips swivelled his head, lizard-like, along the benches. Looking for allies. Since every player had been disgraced by the visitors, Jimmy or no Jimmy in goals, most kept their eyes on the muddy floor, scuffing their boots, or quietly lifting bottles of shampoo and towels from their kitbags. Tiptoeing to the showers. Only Victor and Dog Breath leered greedily at Hamblin, willing him to step up a gear. As if he needed any encouragement.

'Maybe Kelly was rubbish out there –' Hamblin had a hand up to the side of his mouth, feigning discretion, '– because he's slimming now. Cutting down the old pies and cream cakes makes you weak, so you canny think straight.' The lizard head turned from Jimmy, scanned the benches.

Heads stayed down. Hamblin was dangerous like this. He might be picking on Jimmy right now, but anyone could be next in line for a dose of ritual humiliation.

Two more lads managed to slip behind Hamblin into the showers as he dug deeper.

'Tell me Kelly, d'you not feel a big jessie being the only bloke among all those fat lassies at your slimming club?'

Shaking their heads, several more boys escaped to the showers.

'Give over,' Billy McIndope muttered. A few on the benches sniggered, but only Victor wore a grin that split his face.

Jimmy sighed. He daren't be late for English. First lesson of the new term. Ellie was meeting him outside class so they could sit together.

'Sir,' Jimmy urged, 'I'm not in a slimming club.'

He was wasting his breath.

'What is it they do again? Put you on scales in the scuddy and boo you if you havenae lost anything? Give you a wee clap if you've been good.' Hamblin's slow handclap ricocheted around the changing room.

'I don't go to a slimming club, Sir.'

'You're still a fair bit off your – what d'you call it – "target weight"? Bullseye, eh, lads?'

Hamblin held his whistle poised, dartlike, between

finger and thumb, and aimed at Jimmy's belly. He'd one eye closed. The mime earned him a smattering of laughter and Jimmy could sense a mood of hostility seeping like invisible toxin through the boys remaining on the benches. This was exactly what Hamblin wanted; a great stressbuster for the team.

Déjà vu.

Jimmy's heart sank. Surely it wasn't all going to begin again? Coming to school today, fourth year, new term, he'd felt his life really had turned the corner.

No one had snorted or taken the mick when he got changed today.

He and Findlay McKay, who was new to the swimming squad, had arranged to go to the gym before training.

He'd even made a couple of saves during the match. Everyone, including Victor, applauding him.

The gravest indignity Jimmy had borne since returning to St Jude's was from a lippy wee first year who'd never seen Jimmy before. *Fee Fie Fo Fum,* he chanted after Jimmy in the corridor. He could live with that.

Other lads further up the school had been staring at Jimmy too. But not like before. It was obvious some of them barely recognised him.

'That's yon big bloater, innit?'

'Nah. Fat Kelly wasnae as tall.'

'New guy, then?'

'Must be.'

'Looks like Kelly right enough.'

Girls in the school were clocking Jimmy too, the fleet, approving up and down of their eyes like fingertips tripping the hairs on his skin. Since he became a fourth year he seemed to be blushing a lot more. It *was* embarrassing, mind you, when teachers insisted he was a new sixth year until they checked his name against the class register.

'Jimmy Kelly? It's you. What a transformation!'

No such confusion where Hamblin was concerned. No compliments. He looked at Jimmy and he saw what he wanted to see: a scapegoat, a wheezy pain of a butterball who deserved to be vilified.

'Does your mammy send in wee notes to the

slimming club if you don't lose any weight? *"Dear Fat Controller",'* Hamblin wheedled, pretending his whistle was a pen. *'"Please don't boo my Jimmy. He's been awfy hungry this week".'*

'Sir, I said I don't go to a slimming club.' Jimmy tried to make himself heard above the inevitable caws of laughter that followed Hamblin's insulting impersonation of Mum. He was heart sick of this, anger, not embarrassment turning his face as red as a traffic light.

'My mum doesn't speak like that either,' Jimmy's voice rang out. He shook his head, and turned his back on Hamblin.

'Which mum d'you mean, Kelly?' chimed Victor. In a mocking sing-song voice he added, 'Did you know Kelly's got two mammies, Sir?'

Barry Dyer would have been impressed by the acceleration of Jimmy's dive at Victor. From a standing start he was towering over him, eyes blazing, face so close that he could count Victor's galaxy of blackheads.

'I've really had enough of all this,' Jimmy said, bearing down closer, his hands spread wide on either side of Victor's spotty neck, watching Victor shrink and slide down the changing room wall.

'Stop this –' Hamblin plucked feebly at Jimmy's arm. 'Take your hands off –'

'Haven't touched him. Sir.' Jimmy threw off Hamblin's grip and spun to face him. Hamblin, half a head smaller than Jimmy, took an involuntary step backwards, losing his balance and landing like a deck chair folding on Dog Breath's lap.

'Never been to a slimming club, Sir,' said Jimmy in the same clear voice that had shut Victor up. 'Don't need to. I'm fine the way I am.'

Slinging his towel over his shoulder, Jimmy strode to the showers, head held high.

'Please sir, Jimmy's in a *swimming* club, sir. He's seriously good.'

'*Seriously good,* s'at right McKay?' railed Hamblin, trying to sound posh. 'How would a moron like you know if someone was *seriously good* at anything? You're an even bigger balloon than Kelly. Did you think you were at Murrayfield when you picked the ball up and ran with it? This is *FITBA'*, ye posh dope.'

Findlay MacKay sloped into the shower next to Jimmy, Hamblin bellowing after him, 'MacKay's not the biggest balloon, either. That honour goes to you, Swift. Sitting there, thinking you're camouflaged under all those plukes. You've nothing to laugh about. Swift by name and Swift by nature? Not. No wonder your fancy team dropped you this season.'

'Thanks,' Jimmy spluttered through the water to Findlay McKay.

'Pleasure,' grinned Findlay through a shampoo beard. 'Hamblin's a twally. See you later.'

Jimmy let the water cascade over him, rinsing away Hamblin's scorn before he met Ellie. When he left the showers only Victor remained, head down, shoulderblades up to his ears, face to the wall. As though, thought Jimmy, he wanted to be invisible.

Well, it had been a cruel, cruel summer for Victor Swift, as the song goes. Not only was he out of Barry's swimming squad, 'Permo, Jimmy,' for defacing the Swimathon posters but, as Hamblin had jeered, he'd been dropped from his premier league boys' team.

'Wasn't keeping up his training without Coach on

his back,' Findlay McKay whispered to Jimmy with a nod to the showers.

'Och, that's rough,' said Jimmy, glancing at the lone figure. Jimmy couldn't help himself. Despite everything, he felt sorry for Vic Swift. Over and above all his sporting misfortunes, Victor was undergoing such drastic physical mutations that Jimmy, having been there, done that – albeit in reverse – had to empathise.

Over the summer, Victor had developed chronic acne and his complexion these days was an ever-changing landscape, pitted here, swollen there, erupting everywhere, alive with its own abundant vegetation. It was as though, thought Jimmy, someone had put tomatoes, red peppers, bananas and a handful of purple grapes into a food processor, turned it on without the lid, and stuck Victor's face over it. No wonder, to all bar Dog Breath, he was Nobby No-Mates now; the Leper of St Jude's.

Even Senga, who had stuck by Victor, limpet-like, had had enough. 'Swifty's mingin',' she informed anyone who would listen. 'He's no' touchin' me. Even his plukes have got plukes.'

Today, Jimmy knew only too well, as he left the changing room, Victor was hanging back in the showers deliberately. Until everyone had left. Then he would change alone.

In the corridor, heading for English, Jimmy passed the new noticeboard, and stopped. Remembered GI Joe's photograph was in his bag. Pinned it up, under Ellie's heading:

Father Joseph's Family

The new photograph made a brilliant contrast with the first picture Jimmy had seen of the middle of nowhere: that tumbledown shack. Now it was rebuilt. Underneath *that* was the Bruce Willis photograph. GI Joe, large as life, grinning out at Jimmy, surrounded by all his kids.

Jimmy didn't know why he reached out and touched the photograph, returning GI Joe's grin. Didn't even realise he was doing it until a hand grabbed his wrist.

'Hey. You leave Coach alone.'

Shoulders square to the noticeboard, Jimmy and Victor eyeballed each other. Victor was glaring fiercely, the hand that had grabbed Jimmy laid flat to the photograph on the wall.

'Don't touch that,' he said. 'He wasn't just *your* mate.'

Victor's glare held, but less fierce now.

You really miss him, thought Jimmy, recalling the last time he and Victor had stared at each other like this. The butterfly race. The beginning of the beginning for Jimmy. The beginning of the end for . . .

'Sorry, I was just . . .' Jimmy shrugged, breaking the eyelock. He stepped back. 'Magic new picture,' he grinned, pointing out GI Joe's smart roof. Then he left the noticeboard free for Victor.

'By the way,' called Jimmy, walking backwards up the corridor. 'Coach was asking for you. Use it or lose it, he said I've to tell you. Have you written to him yet?'

Jimmy wasn't sure of Victor's reply. If there was one. He didn't really care.

Ellie was standing outside Mrs Hughes' room.

Waiting. For him.